The Tobacco Barn

A Novel

Tennessee Gunns

BURKWOOD
Media Group

Burkwood Media Group, PO Box 29448, Charlotte, NC 28229

www.burkwoodmedia.com

Printed in the United States of America

ISBN: 978-0-578-61399-4

Dedication

Clifford "Petom" Green (1972 - 2018)
With love and admiration.

Acknowledgements

Countless people deserve special recognition for their support during the writing of this book. I would like to thank my wife, Debra, who is not only an exemplary mother but has provided much love and support during my extensive writing sessions. My sincerest gratitude for your understanding.

Thank you to my oldest son, Drew Lester, who gave valuable feedback on both the book and characters. Your brilliance will take you places.

Thanks to my youngest son, Carson Lester, whose entrepreneurial spirit inspired me to dream big.

To my cool sibling, Angela, my witty father, Larry, and my encouraging mother, Donna, I offer much gratitude and great appreciation. My hat goes off to my grandfather, Tippie, for his friendship and also to the rare soul who was my grandmother, Pearl.

To Mr. Bailey, a great teacher of history.

To a host of friends and family, thank you for your laughs and friendship.

A special thanks goes to my editors Cherilyn Basbano and Holland Webb.

Finally, thank you Debra Funderburk and the team at Burkwood Media, Charlotte, North Carolina for your assistance and patience during this wonderful journey.

I

Coming Home, 1948

Wrapping a thin blue sweater around her shoulders, Annie walked to the end of Tobacco Road. She opened the rusty brown mailbox and placed three letters inside. The envelopes, sealed by her daughter's hand, were heading to the other side of the world. Drops of morning dew fell to the ground when the lid to the mailbox slammed closed. She raised the red metal flag and shuffled through a handful of mail, uncovering a delivery her daughter would be especially pleased to read. Annie's steps were slower back to the farmhouse as she continued browsing the envelopes.

Annie picked a handful of yellow and white lilies for her breakfast table as she stopped to watch the American Paint Horses in full gait moving across the neighbor's pasture behind the tall and wide oaks that lined their property. The peeping of baby birds high in their nests made her smile because spring finally was in the air. The farm was in full bloom, and nature was precious to her. Her eyes squinted as she snatched a glimpse of the beautiful sun making its way to warm the day in Savannah.

Like a good mother, Annie instilled her respect for nature and a love of wildlife in her daughter, Nedra.

"Nedra, the Lord has carved out little treasures and spread them all around us," expressed Annie.

"Mama, that's why we love living out here," Nedra nodded in agreement.

Whitetail deer residing along the property's trails and numerous coveted features made the Randolph's land desirable. Nedra soaked up the early morning light while gazing out her bedroom window. When Nedra was big enough to keep up with her mother, the two would hike the winding trails behind the tobacco barn and explore nature. The lush fields of blooming flowers could supply the whole state of Georgia if needed. The land around the farmhouse was a work of art and brought about a sense of pride for the Randolphs. Nedra swept a strand of fallen bangs away from her eyes and touched a letter addressed from the soldier she loved serving in Korea. Annie paused to watch her daughter muscle up the aged window from the second floor of their lowcountry home.

"Any letters for me, Mama?" Nedra asked as she poked her head outside.

Her mother waved a letter signaling that Nedra had something from Korea.

"You got another letter from that boy!"

Nedra pulled herself back inside and tucked the white curtains to each side of the hooks. Her sandy brown hair bounced as she jetted to her mother's side with eagerness.

"That boy must really like you. This letter must be a month old." Annie held the envelope up to the sunlight. She tucked the lilies inside a vase and shuffled her favorite letters to the top, stacking them neatly in order.

Nedra raced to her room to finish brushing her hair and humming her way outside past her father's work area to her secret spot in the loft of the tobacco barn, where she read her letters repeatedly. Nedra kept a shoebox full of his handwritten love letters, some cut with a letter opener and others ripped from the end, all hidden in a wooden trunk covered in dried flowers and hay bales. She folded a red and black plaid blanket spread out so she could relax, kicking up her heels on the hay to read the letters while looking out across the wildflower fields and trails.

The cool morning breeze off the Georgia coast, chilled her pale Irish skin. She closed her eyes and imagined how she'd soon disappear with Mickey down one of the trails when her soldier returned home. Mickey never missed a day of writing and daydreaming of Nedra, who had filled four shoeboxes in less than a year. Once, the Army had taken Mickey across the world to stand guard in Japan. This letter, however, would be his first from Korea. Gazing out the loft, Nedra watched her father, Daniel, step from rock to rock, dodging the muddy ground as he walked from the tobacco barn back to the farmhouse. Her father's voice was deep and defined, his hands were worn and cut from building the barn, and his actions were purposeful.

"Annie, got any mail for me?" he joked and leaned in to kiss his wife.

"No, Daniel, but you could do me a favor if you are going to town, though."

"Sorry, dear, I'm not headed to town today, I've got to clear a place for the car in the back of the barn." He hung his keys to the car and the barn on a hook by the kitchen door. "I'll be finished by summer's end just in time to start selling tobacco in the fall."

Daniel poured his second cup of coffee for the morning. He gently sipped the top of the dark coffee, making a slurping sound. "Ahhhh. I put a bid on a few truckloads of tobacco leaves from North Carolina and a few from Connecticut. It looks like I have a long list of customers who want tobacco when it arrives." He grinned and nodded. "I hope this boy Mickey Starr is home in time to help us unload trucks this fall."

Annie gazed at Daniel, who was busy eating breakfast. "Our daughter's upstairs now reading another letter from him. Mickey left Japan; the letter was sent from Korea." Pouring more coffee into Daniel's cup, she continued. "It's going to be a long summer of letters between him and Nedra."

"Heck of a worker, that Mickey," said Daniel.

"Not a bad singer either," replied Annie, smiling.

"He can play the guitar, and he can work on engines."

At nightfall, Nedra made herself comfortable in her bed and swiftly tucked away the letters when she heard her mother's footsteps creaking up the stairs.

Annie knocked at the door. "Can I come in?"

"It's open."

Her mother took a seat at the end of the bed. "How's Mickey?"

"Mama, I'm afraid for him." Nedra closed her eyes and reached for her mother.

"Your daddy was asking about him at breakfast," Annie spoke softly while stroking her daughter's hand.

"He did?" Her face looked in awe, while she held her mother's hand.

"Your dad prayed for him to come home and help with tobacco this fall."

Nedra sat up tall in her bed. "Mickey would love to help with the barn." She hugged her mother and squealed with delight.

"I know your daddy likes him, don't worry."

"I was worried. What daddy thinks is important to me. I wouldn't want to disappoint him."

Annie rested her hand on Nedra's leg. "He was in the Army, remember? He understands how dangerous it can be in a combat zone."

"I love him, Mama." Nedra sighed deeply and slumped back into her pillow.

"I know, sweetheart. I can tell," said Annie as she arose from the bed and left the bedroom. "I checked the mail every day when your dad was overseas."

***

Mickey would pen a letter every chance he had to write a few paragraphs, tucking the notes away into his uniform pocket. The moon's glow would reflect just enough light off the freshly fallen snow for him to finish a letter and seal it before he closed his eyes each night.

Dearest Nedra,

I imagine you are likely reading this letter in the loft of the tobacco barn nestled in the beautiful spot you often write. The place where you look out over the flower fields and see the pheasants flying and your neighbor's horses trotting around the pastureland. I miss you, and love you very much. I hope to get home to you soon.

Tomorrow, we take Hill 180, what I would give to have a canteen full of your daddy's hot coffee in this frigid snowstorm. It's beautiful at times, and the roads remind me of the trails we walked together. Other times it's scary and deadly, I'm not afraid to admit that to you. I tried to pray yesterday, as you said. It felt strange when I talked to the Lord, and I'm not sure if it worked anyway. Although it's hard to tell if it helped, I'm alive, so there is a possibility. I hope the strong faith you have in God will save me, and how you pray for me makes me feel good about us.

I don't think the Army will honorably discharge a soldier for being lovesick, so I'll try my best to push forward. All I think about is getting home to you. You are the most beautiful girl in the world, and since I've been around the world, I can say that is true. Anyway, I want to see us together and get married soon, maybe next year. I can't wait to hold you in my arms and kiss you again. I love you.

All my love,

Private Mickey Starr

A handful of hours into his rest, Mickey woke to bombs exploding on a nearby hillside. The heat from the flames peered through the window. Soldiers took cover, and some of his buddies ran across the hill in the wake of another attack. The land was on fire, and chaos ensued. It was then that Private Starr witnessed two of his best buddies die within an hour of one another. Sickened by the somber reality of a bloody war, Mickey missed his hometown of Savannah. His greatest desire was to see Nedra again and speak to her father.

2

Tybee Island Pier, 1995

Four decades had passed since the war in Korea, and a flashlight Mickey used to write Nedra letters from Korea flickered and soon lost its glow. The bulb needed replacing, Mickey thought. He sat on the high dunes just before daybreak, anticipating a long day. Sage grass moved behind him, providing a slight distraction from his morning ritual. A message or sign could offer a pretense of hope, while his bare feet submerged beneath the sand. The waves were rougher than usual as storms shattered the south. Another one was headed to the coast of Georgia. Mickey prepared his mind for a hard couple of weeks when the storm would make landfall, a picture of disaster he'd seen many times in his forty years as a commercial fisherman. The sheer gravity of the impending weather-controlled his thoughts, doubling him over at night resembling the terror he felt as a young man, marching off to war. He spent much of the drive with dread churning in his belly as each looming thought of what the weather could do, sickened him. The aftermath of hurricanes and storm surges made him feel helpless, and out of control, a golf ball-sized lump rested in this throat. Desperate to hatch a promising back up plan, coffee and his favorite Fuente cigar, brought comfort to him as he gripped one in each hand.

For now, his watercraft were safe at the harbor, in pristine condition, as he naturally preferred. Calm. He had twenty of the finest fishing boats in the south, docked and adorned in red lettering, 'Starr Fishing Company - Whitemarsh Island, Georgia,' separating his fleet from other vessels in the harbor. A sudden updraft sprayed him with sand forcing his eyes shut. Mickey recovered and staggered across the sand to the nearby boardwalk where he heard the voice of a lady echoing from the Tybee Island pier. Mickey stood and sang the words of a familiar country song. The lady's tenor voice matched the melody as he nodded his head and moved in her direction.

"Sarah, I like that song," Mickey said as he waved, making his way over to her.

"Why Mickey Starr, it has been years," Sarah proclaimed, dropping her guitar and reaching for her old friend.

"Twenty years, maybe?" He always gave a bear hug to his close friends. She was petite and spun around easily.

"Twenty at least, maybe more." Her soft kiss braised his cheek.

"It has been decades, dear." He stood beside her against the rail. "Too long." He looked at her and caught her smile. "Sing that song again."

Sarah winked at him. "Anything for you, sweetheart," pulling her guitar back around her shoulder, she pointed to the inside of her used guitar case.

Mickey placed a sizable bill inside the red velour-lined guitar case that reeked of beer and cigarettes. Sarah's green eyes had taken on a strange stare across the water, and she sang as if her mind was somewhere else.

He signaled his goodbye with a slow wave when the song was over, walking back to his favorite spot in the sand. Runners dodged the tide as two fishermen struck up a conversation with Mickey, chatting when he could with friends on the island, and he enjoyed seeing vacationers gobble up seafood he'd caught with his boats.

His spirit had been broken many times from hardships caused by storms. He anticipated something more was out there as he found his seat in the sand, questioning the idea of faith and generally distanced himself from the chapel. The Lord didn't speak to him much, and he never quite understood why. The fisherman chose to follow his path, a simple one made up of cryptic messages or signs that he felt fate handed him. Life threw him a few unwanted curves causing an onslaught of unanswered questions. Wondering what was next on his list of disasters, Mickey smoked his cigar. Long overdue, he accepted but still thought some good news would be helpful in light of his weathered personal storms over the past few years.

Boating and fishing were his blood right, his legacy, an opportunity for which he was most grateful. And yet, especially in times like these, he felt hollow. It was as if he secretly yearned for something more. As much as fishing fulfilled him financially and directly contributed to the well-being of many families on his crew, still, with all of his success, Mickey felt uneasy. Perhaps it's unfulfillment.

His thoughts re-centered, "How spoiled and entitled could one man be?" Mickey's mind continued the battle, "Am I incapable of feeling satisfaction? Or completeness?" He attributed his drive to be successful and hunger to have more, as the lifeline of his lucrative fishing business was in the line.

Convinced that believing otherwise would seem unfit and ill-deserving, Mickey felt tired or defeated, rocked by nature and trials of life. He discovered solace on the sea but longed for more of something to occupy the rest of his years. Something was eating at him. Worried sick about the pending storm, Mickey wondered if the world had something else to offer him as he questioned having poured his heart and soul into the fishing industry. The love of the water kept him busy and unsatisfied. He wondered whether he should have cashed out years ago.

Once, a wealthy man from Odessa offered him a large share to command an oil venture, but he wouldn't commit to leaving the coast of Georgia for Texas. Investing in a diamond mine in West Africa crossed his desk in '83, he remembered the letter and the month. The offers were there, good ones, strange as they seemed for a popular man. Mickey continued to revel in regret of possible missed signs, missed messages, missed opportunities. He was pissed about what he'd declined. With all of the wild and precarious offers, Mickey couldn't commit to a new endeavor. So, by default, he felt the sea would provide him what he needed. A worn bottle propped up in the sand with a message inside would be a rare treasure to find, he once said.

He would rarely go anywhere alone since his wife, his best friend, Nedra, passed the year before. Today though, he was with his sidekick and faithful grandson, Tipp Starr, a stout young man at twenty-two, fit as a fiddle. Sometimes he wondered what it would be like to chart his own course and career path, far and away from commercial fishing.

His grandfather stationed himself in his favorite spot beside Tipp and ruffled the boy's shaggy blonde hair, which was his typical greeting for his grandson despite the way it aggravated the devil out of Tipp.

"Who's the lady with the guitar?" Tipp combed his hair down with his hands. His grandfather unearthed a shark's tooth and tucked it inside his shirt pocket. Finally, some good luck, he felt.

His grandfather found the lady in his sight again. "She was a friend I met long before your grandma, of course."

"Well, I didn't think any different," said Tipp, laughing and tossing shells into the pounding waves.

Mickey frowned. "Her mind is gone, though."

"What happened?" inquired Tipp, glancing back at the singer as he listened.

"Too much pain to numb."

Mickey and Tipp both waved one last time as she nodded in acknowledgment while playing and singing to the small group of gawking tourists. The storm was due to hit Savannah soon, so Tipp missed a full night's sleep to escort his grandfather to the shore before sunup. As he separated broken seashells from sand and skipped sand dollars across the tide, Tipp admired a woman on the pier. He straightened himself to appear more stoic. He wished his grandfather wasn't in tow.

Mickey sighed. "With this storm on the way, makes me wish I had gone into cleanup versus growing the family's seafood business. This will be a gold mine for a cleanup crew but a bad time to be a fisherman." He drew air back into his lungs and closing his eyes; he slowly seeped the air out of his nostrils. The air resonated in and out. Mickey experienced anxiety when he felt shaken by uncertainties and unresolved issues.

Tipp witnessed the old man's unorthodox approach to dealing with life, storms, and numerous deeper issues. The locals considered Mickey southern royalty, and his word was golden in the south. He was proud of his grandfather and had learned to accept his ways.

Tipp's deep voice reminded Mickey of his father, Emrick Starr. He'd learned from him the importance of knowing when to lead and who to follow, mentioning things like fishing and good coffee, and filling a tobacco pipe. Or better yet, how to be a man.

Mickey appreciated Tipp's company just as much as Tipp enjoyed hanging out with him. The duo was practically inseparable, but they had their bouts and disagreements.

"Grandpa, do you mind if we speed this up a bit?" asked Tipp, grunting, and grumbling. "I'm too tired and hungry to be mindful or ponder about the storm any longer. Let's get something to eat. Men think better at breakfast, anyway."

Tipp affectionately called his grandfather, Grandpa, but was known for calling him Mickey in front of friends or as an attention grabber. Other times, he did it to piss him off.

"Coffee, Mickey?" Tipp asked, reaching him a thermos.

"One more cup will hold me." The two shared the dark coffee. Mickey leaned toward the ocean and focused, in deep thought, on the tide. "What I'd give for a good sign."

***

Herman Starr, Mickey's grandfather, and his father, Emrick, genetically injected shots of intellectual inheritance to be passed down to all descendants. At age twelve, Mickey began his apprenticeship alongside these two fishing greats, known beyond the waters of Savannah. Mickey had grown to love his seashore town as much as he loved sneaking tobacco from his Papaw Herman's Mail Pouch bag.

The last conversation Mickey had with his grandfather, with great sincerity, he said, "Papaw Herman, I want to be just like you when I grow up."

"Don't be like me, Mickey," he said, throwing up his hands. "Be better than me. Be much better than I am," said Herman, handing him five dollars. "Don't make greedy decisions like me; learn to be a good man, a selfless man."

Emotions rang like a dinner bell whenever Mickey thought back to his grandfather's words and how he longed to see him again. He wanted to be like him. His soul ached when he thought of the loss of his prized loved ones, and the loneliness developed as a result.

Lifting one eyebrow, Mickey, turned to his sleepy grandson. "I'd like to have another go-round in this life," jingling seashells in his hand. "Knowing good people might save your life." Tipp wasn't sure why his grandfather was so melancholy, but he understood that the old man had a lot on his mind. Not to mention a lot to lose. Fear amplified Mickey's anxiety causing him to bounce back and forth between trains of thought.

After turning his family business into a fortune, industry folks nicknamed this seafood baron 'The Son of the South,' a notable name that stuck but one that Mickey didn't enjoy hearing. At times, Mickey felt the title was too extravagant; other times, the responsibility divided his heart about individual business decisions over the years. Mickey struggled with upcoming decisions, dictating that he make choices that will have him choosing between his community and himself.

Tipp squinted his eyes. "You've been dulled by the punches of life. You'll get it back."

"That would imply that I lost it?" smiled Mickey. "Oh, I've still got it, young grasshopper. I've still got it." He laughed. "I'll show you that I still got it."

Drifting back to his meditation for a moment, Mickey, tilted his head and focused his eyes on the crushing waves at Tybee Island. He scanned the horizon for something extraordinary. Mickey took another deep breath and sighed, inhaling and exhaling slowly. Scenarios flipped through his mind about what he would do with so many people on the payroll and a fleet destroying storm thundering in the Atlantic Ocean, targeting its power on historic Savannah.

"Tipp, there's only a handful of things a man cannot control in his life."

"Like what?"

"Women, weather, and pit bulls," Mickey chuckled at his joke.

Tipp grabbed his belly, "Pit bulls, huh? Good one." Hearing someone approach, the two saw a long-haired man stumbling up behind them. After catching his breath by propping himself up against the wooden piling, the man continued staggering down the ramp. The stranger's Italian leather belt held up his slacks

16

covering his thin-framed body. Wire rimmed glasses shaped his aging eyes. The man's dress shoes matched his belt and tie, but scuff marks appeared on the wingtips.

Widening his eyes, Mickey cocked his head as the man seemed eerily familiar, imagining what he, himself, would turn just like this man if he couldn't get a handle on his drinking. He locked eyes with the drunk, and it was as if he was staring into a mirror for a moment. Rubbing his eyes, while sighing deeply, his concern for the other person was obvious, and remembered what his grandfather taught him about being generous. He composed himself and cleared his throat to gain the man's attention. His wrinkled hand hid a bagged bottle. Mickey stepped in after watching the man struggle with his footing, being careful not to spill the man's drink on his clothes.

Witnessing the unsettling voice of the stranger, Tipp said, "Let's do this guy a favor and help him to the shade under the pier." Mickey patted his grandson on the back. The two of them carefully grabbed the man under each arm and hoisted him over by the pier, cleaning his high-dollar shoes of sand for him.

"It's good to see you," said the unshaven drunkard. "Been a while, huh?"

Mickey comforted Tipp regarding the man. "Don't worry, he'll sober up soon; he just needs to sleep it off."

Removing an ink pen from the drunk man's shirt pocket, Mickey hesitated as he stood. Tipp watched as his grandfather scribbled on a torn section of a brown paper bag, tucking the pen and the note inside the man's pocket.

"What did you write on the note?" asked Tipp, rubbing his chin. "Why did you leave him a message in the first place?"

"He's a good man, a real good man. Grady Johnson is his name. I've known him my whole life, and this is not as it seems. I like this guy; he did me a favor once," Mickey explained, adjusting Grady's drunken body to a more comfortable position and adjusting his tie. In the reclined position under the pier, the man clutched his shirt pocket and drifted off to sleep. Tipp walked toward the truck, hoping to get the old man loaded up and to the nearest food bar.

"Breakfast time, my boy, the ham and eggs are calling my name." Mickey stood tall against the unknown and scanned the horizon one last time. He trekked quickly to the end of the pier and mumbled to himself, "What shall I do?"

Tipp examined his grandfather's suntanned hands. The old man pulled thoughts out of his salt and pepper goatee while he watched the seagulls nearby. Mickey squinted as the first rays of sunshine broke behind a stack of clouds, snapping his fingers as his lips missed a sip of his strong coffee. He wiped the wetness from his shirt with his hand, then drummed his fingers against his heart.

"The mystery of people fires me up," Mickey chimed in. He gently tugged his ear. "I'd just stay in bed if all people were mean and ugly. I'd hide my face under the covers if a grudge was the best I had to give away. "It's the good that keeps me going," he smiled. "Everyday heroes, the ordinary who do the extraordinary, that's the gas in my tank," Mickey spoke somberly, glancing at his protege.

"A higher power, you mean?" asked Tipp.

"Why do you spend so much damn time trying to get me to believe in folklore?"

"It's not folklore." Tipp turned his body to the other side of the pier.

"Seems to me like y'all can't decide who you want to believe. You have Santa giving out presents and the Easter Bunny hiding eggs. And all of this deception takes place at church. That makes no sense to me," said the old man. "If the man upstairs is real, then why do you spend so much time and energy on this unnecessary folklore? Deceiving children is, well, inconceivable. Counterintuitive. Religion is part propaganda and part hypocrisy, and I want no part of that." Mickey tilted his head and shrugged his shoulders. He angled his body in Tipp's direction and paused for a rebuttal.

"It's not propaganda," Tipp answered, raking the windblown hair from his face. "The Good Book is the truth, that's all I can say."

Mickey said frowning. "Tipp, I don't think you're winning this argument. Good thing you didn't go to college for law. I believe I've got you on this one."

"I will win you over. Someday you will see the truth, old man, you will see." Tipp patted his grandfather's shoulder, assuring him.

"If the Lord is real, prove it!" Mickey threw a seashell off the pier into the waves.

"He will," Tipp announced in confidence.

Mickey backed down. "You are just like your grandma."

The rough waves thunderously crashed under the pier as if it were a warning for his harsh words. Mickey's eyes widened, tapping his chin, he pondered.

"Are you sweating?" Tipp shook his head in an unsettling way.

"I tried talking to God, at least for a while. I begged Him to save my sick wife, and He turned his back on her and on me too. When I saw my sweet loving, God-fearing Nedra being destroyed by cancer, my faith left me." He waved his hands as if emptying them. "Oh, I prayed, I begged, I bartered, but nothing happened." Mickey pulled his cap down tighter onto his sun-scorched head.

"I can't explain pain, suffering, or even death, but God is real," answered Tipp. "That's what faith is about. I can't see Him, but He's real. His spirit is with us."

"Faith, huh?" Mickey put his hands down, "Well, since you know Him so well, go ahead and put in an order for me. I'll have a serving of miracle with a side of faith to turn this storm around." Mickey responded mockingly with a smirk.

The old man headed toward his truck, stepping down onto the sandy walkway. Mickey kicked at a small pile of sand frustrated by the day's conversation and the horrible events about to unfold. Both of them slapped the bottoms of their shoes together like chalkboard erasers, and Tipp slipped on his before entering Mickey's classic truck.

"Let's go eat," said Mickey, chuckling. "I want some Easter bunny eggs and buttered toast." The old man turned, grinning at Tipp as he found his keys.

The worst storm in ages was about to unleash its wrath on the Great South. Mickey continued to follow his one-part hippie, one part independent, destiny driven path. The widower was generally upbeat and positive until Nedra's death emotionally depleted him. Nothing Tipp could say could restore him. Mickey could never recover from his pain.

***

"The ocean is like summer love." Mickey shifted gears. "Soft, gentle sunsets in an unforgettable backdrop coupled with an

21

alluring fragrance. That stuff sticks in my mind forever, no matter how far I trail from her." The way Mickey described the sea showed what love he had for the waterways. "Savannah intrigues me that way, like the sensual way a woman tugs on your shirt to let you know she wants a deeper, longer embrace. She's quietly controlling and peaceful at times, unpredictable and destructive." Mickey chuckled. "I can't ever drift away from this place; it's serenity for me. All of my memories are here. I would never forgive myself if I forgot one single memory of my beloved Nedra, even as I age, I will never forget. That's why I chose to call Savannah home."

Mickey would continue riding an emotional roller coaster. At times, he was angry about losing his wife, other times worried about the storm and his crew, worried about his fleet, worried about his bottom line. Mickey seemed to hide this side of him amongst friends. He felt safe, with Tipp, he showed his somber and reflective side.

His grandfather's eyes never unlocked from the coast. Tipp followed Mickey's every action and clung to his every word since he was a young boy. The old man meant the world to him as Mickey was his surrogate father and mother. Tipp even liked how he would stroke his long goatee when he had something brewing in his mind.

"I bet you have a hundred stories to tell, don't you?" Tipp rolled the bill of his cap. Mickey's mouth cracked a slight smile. Hidden away in the memory bank was a treasure trove of stories he could expel if only he would. Tipp tried manipulating him back to his storytelling mode to brighten his mood a little. The old man was a gifted wordsmith who found great pleasure in sharing most of them. Tipp punched Mickey's shoulder to get him to elaborate, a daunting task since Nedra died.

His mind faded to younger days, a time even before marriage, a time where Nedra ventured to the harbor and stayed the weekend wrapped in a blanket on the beach. Her parents thought she was with her friends on Miller Street. The memory was so vivid. He must have replayed it a hundred times over, especially when the stores would start selling flowers and candy for Valentine's Day. The fisherman was a cupcake when it came to taking care of Nedra and offering her sentiments and letters. He concluded his reminiscing and said, "Isn't it strange how something so beautiful can also be a source of so much comfort and yet so much pain?"

"I know," Tipp agreed with noticeably misty eyes.

"The locals are heading to the high country--bailing out for fear of what the sea will bring to town. Not me, I'm staying put, just can't leave my boats and my home behind." Mickey examined the calmness of water along highway 80. "The sea giveth, and the sea taketh away. Familiar words to you, huh, boy?" Rubbing his chest and arching his back, the driver took a series of shallow breaths and held it.

"You alright, Grandpa?" Tipp leaned close, reaching for his arm.

"Gas pain," he pressed again. "It's just indigestion."

"I think more than gas pains this time. You don't look so good."

"I'm alright, Doctor Tipp. Simmer down now."

His grandson snatched the cigar from his mouth. "Give me that!" Tipp took the stogie without much of a fight, extinguishing it, and tossed it to the floorboard. "Are you kidding me, old man? Cancer took grandma Nedra's life, and I'm not going to let it take yours, too!"

"I'm fine, boy." He relaxed his eyes as the color in his face slowly returned to normal. "I'm alright."

Fretting about the chest pain, Mickey felt his blood pressure might be the culprit due to the added stress of the impending storm. Although the pain had only come to him once before, he was relieved to have Tipp nearby. Anxious about his health churned his own storm and concerns inside. Boats. Payroll. Crew. Trying to change the tone, he gripped the steering wheel. "A good man has to live each day with ripe anticipation." He glanced over at Tipp. "I've invested a lifetime in these boats. Breaks my heart to lose even a lure in the water."

"Yep, lots of money," said Tipp. "Speaking of providing, I need to eat."

***

Tipp was young and inexperienced of the world, but he was no fool. A smart, college graduate, mature for his age, but he needed direction on his career. Mickey recruited him after graduation to help with management and the new GPS tracking systems. The upgrades to the office were switching from paper logs to computers. His grandfather, the nonconformist, had no choice to convert. He revered the past; the old ways of doing things were better. The spread of the new computer age was not daunting for an old-timer, upgrades, however, were essential to his commercial fishing business.

The Starr name had appeared on boat hulls for two centuries. The fishing industry became renowned, which was a double-edged sword at times. He loved the luxuries that seafood had provided and bragged that the sea should be empty because of all the fish he'd netted. The lavish lifestyle afforded him the means to dream big, and he did. He poured his heart, soul, and bank account into surrounding himself with things he loved. Nedra accepted this about Mickey but was not into collectibles or classic cars. She was conservative, preferring time over tangibles. Mickey spoiled her with gifts each month, and she let him because it made him a happy man. Nedra understood that his purchasing proclivity came from a place of love and not greed. Together they balanced harmoniously, but stumbled on occasion.

"Nervousness haunts me," Mickey said, gripping the steering wheel until his knuckles turned white, and his face turned red.

"Don't let it get to you. No sense worrying about something that hasn't happened yet, something that might not even happen. What a waste of energy. Besides, that's what insurance is for," replied Tipp, trying to calm the mood as he lowered his sunglasses on his nose.

"This is the largest number of boats the Starr family has ever had on the water," said Mickey as he shifted gears nearing the stoplight. "Best damn crew I've ever had too." His concern was hard to shake.

"Lean not on your own understanding," Tipp answered assuredly. "In all your ways acknowledge Him, and He will lead your path."

"I can't bear the thought of going without. Don't want to see my workers go without a paycheck, either." Mickey banged the steering wheel with his fist in frustration.

"They won't," Tipp reassured him, trying to lighten the tone while doing his best to suppress his own dread of what was to come.

"I care deeply for those guys. Come tomorrow morning; they'll all show up to work and look to me for answers." He reached for the radio while he drove, as a distraction.

"You will have them." Tipp supported the old man but was worried about the toll it would take on him tonight. He was familiar with how Mickey dealt with surmounting stressors.

Tipp's front row ticket to watch Mickey's booze-infused frenzy while mourning his grandma's death still plagued his thoughts.

His grandfather lamented further about the storm, and Tipp's suspicions about him drinking to keep from thinking would soon prove true. The empty bottle drained his grandfather's confidence, and yet, Mickey felt, it helped him gain it back, popping the clutch and gripping the shifter like a race car driver on the Atlanta Motor Speedway.

Tipp watched his grandfather's hand reaching toward the ashtray for his favorite smoke, a Fuente cigar from Tampa. Mickey caught a smirk out of the corner of his eye from his grandson.

"You've given them work for years now, provided for a lot of people. Nothing will change."

"Not without boats, I can't."

Both fishermen weathered years of experience with hurricanes striking the east coast; Mickey was nervous about this one. Each was unique, bringing its own particular misery. This storm, however, would prove exceptionally taxing for the Starr family as it's the first storm they would navigate without Nedra and her prayers. The loveable lady was an ace with storm tracking and prayers, a natural at it, and a prayer warrior, too. Tipp teased his grandmother about missing her calling as hurricane tracker, having unnatural 'mermaid tendencies.' Still, Nedra's comprehension of science and nature was a marvel to witness in front of the television. The fisherman had learned to lean on Nedra for storm tracking. Together they were an excellent storm fighting duo, he would drink, and she would predict paths, shouting out her nicknames for storms. It worked. Mickey loved it.

Back at Mickey's Whitemarsh Island mansion, the two men watched the latest weather report just before bed: "Tropical Storm has its eye on Savannah," reported the weatherman.

"Tracking this model will be a rough ride after dark," he predicted.

The wind whistled like a freight train as the rain seared the sky. Trees swayed and snapped across Whitemarsh Island. Like many others, Mickey didn't sleep much. Worried, he kept imagining his fleet battered by the relentless tide and ferocious wind. Consumed by a recurring vision of a single fishing boat bobbing in the water with a piece of mangled rope hanging from the bow, heightened his anxiety. As in years past, he could physically feel the waves swallow each vessel. A stream of bubbles trailed from the last ship as it sank deeper into the depths of the dark ocean. His ships surrendered to the wrath of the storm. The old man wasn't sure if he was having a nightmare or experiencing a premonition. His heart was empty, and his soul felt lost. Collecting his thoughts, he shuffled down the hall, staggering to the other side of the mansion. Halfway, he pressed the wall to gain balance, and mumbled, rolling his eyes, "Far too much to drink."

"Stop hiding my damn tobacco!" he continued to murmur purposely, "I'm a full-grown man." George, his butler had left town for the day. Mickey slammed and cussed every drawer and cabinet in his house, from the kitchen to the car bays. He continued to search the home and added stronger language with each room of his exploration.

Tipp ignored him and smiled.

3

The Switch

The Starr family had fished the waters since the first settlers landed in Savannah. Tipp didn't fully understand his grandfather's passion for fishing, but he did enjoy hearing all the Starr family stories. Working in the fishing industry was not on Tipp's radar. His role in the business was minimal, by choice, as he was the least committed of the crew. Tipp didn't go to college to work for the family business. Instead, he graduated and came home to help, a role that Mickey assumed was permanent, but Tipp assumed temporary.

The howling wind slapped a shutter loose and whipped it wildly against the side of the mansion. Tipp startled from a deep sleep. The wind continued whistling outside, and water beat against the seam of the door. The old man's voice rang in Tipp's mind, and he couldn't shake his worry.

"Nedra's gone, fishing's soon over, and my son doesn't give a damn about any of this," Mickey wailed in drunken despair. "This storm will be the demise of my legacy."

Overhearing his grandfather's voice echoing deep from the great room, Tipp had an epiphany concerning responsibility and obligation. The sudden shift of thought forever changed

Tipp that night. His college days of goofing off and his half-assed response to life came to a halt as a response to his grandfather's desperation that only he could resolve. "Not on my watch," Tipp whispered to himself as he walked down the long corridor.

He continued to hear his grandfather's broken voice from upstairs. "We're not done," said Tipp, gripping the rail and feeling the heaviness of his family's legacy rest on his shoulders. His father returned to his camp in Africa after Nedra passed away, leaving him as the next of kin, by default.

Although he didn't understand Mickey's inner turmoil over the aptly insured fishing vessels, Tipp's stomach was in knots about his grandfather. Still, he felt there had to be something more going on with the old man. Pondering at what he had seen and heard, a temporary hold on incoming funds while settling with the insurance company inevitably won't lead to the dismissal of a family's legacy.

Mickey and Tipp refused to evacuate. Their neighbors thought they were foolish fishermen. Tipp prayed for the storm to pass over while Mickey drank to escape the reality of his long-time investment and livelihood.

Tipp shook his grandfather's leg. "Get up! The worst of the storm has passed. We lost power."

"Kick the generator," moaned Mickey.

"Already did. Get up and let's go check out the boats. I'll make the coffee," offered Tipp. "A strong cup of hot joe will bring you back to normal." Tipp paced across the kitchen to make fresh brew.

"Coffee's good, thanks." Mickey gave the usual thumbs up when Tipp handed him the hot coffee. "Get my boots," he ordered.

Tipp grabbed a thermos of coffee for the road. Mickey would need a refill to jumpstart his broken state if it was as severe as the news predicted. The 'Son of the South' felt like crawling under the sofa, but Tipp helped him to his pickup.

Along the way, Mickey began sobering up just enough to witness the storm damage to Whitemarsh Island. Trees and houses were scattered like fallen dominos along the highway and coastal waterway. The storm had snapped power lines and spread Spanish tiles all onto the streets. Carports were wrapped around tree trunks, and debris was strewn heavily about. The internal damage of homes and businesses remained hidden behind loosened plywood. Mickey took a deep breath, looking out the window.

"Police are directing traffic." Tipp leaned on the wheel, pointing at the soldiers. "National Guard's in town," glancing back and forth at Mickey's long face as he spoke. "Even called in the Army Reserve. Looks like all we need are a few good Marines and the Navy, and Savannah will be safe and locked down."

"Looks like they found us."

"Wow!" Tipp wheeled the truck. "They got here fast. Unbelievable how things can change in less than 24 hours."

"Everything is destroyed, I bet," said Mickey, gripping his head and scanning the highway.

Tipp trucked through the muddy roadway. Mickey spotted one of his boats on the street with the busted bow. "That's one of mine," claimed the old man as he faded back into the seat. Mickey couldn't look; he spent the rest of the drive burying his head in his hands. Tipp shifted gears and said, "Finish your coffee."

Mickey slumped further down into his seat, covering his eyes with his green Army hat. He simply couldn't face anymore devastation. His faithful grandson rushed to the marina, parked, and trekked his way to the ramp. He passed a dozen of Mickey's brand-new boats, destroyed with fragments deposited all over the marina parking lot. The access road was partially blocked, forcing Tipp to move some of the downed limbs.

Staring across Bull River, Mickey shouted in desperation, "Damn, you storm!"

Tipp sat on what was left of a wooden dock and collected himself. Deciding how to disclose the information to his grandfather, Tipp adjusted his long pants and spat into the murky water. Returning to the truck, Tipp neglected eye contact as he climbed back inside the cab.

"I can't believe they're all gone. Every single boat we have.... had," said Tipp, correcting himself.

Mickey stepped out and hurled his thermos against the remnants of one of his boats. The old man collapsed to his knees, surrounded by muck. A child's baby doll washed up, further sobering the moment. Several orange life vests floated by along with a broken oar. A half-submerged ice chest rested in his eyeshot. Mickey used the ice chest as a make-shift stool, grabbed the oar, and stood it on end to rest his chin. He found it hard to stand, hard to breathe, hard to see.

"This looks like.... well, this must be what war looks like." Tipp shook his head in dismay. "I've never seen anything like it." The young man crushed his hat in sadness as he covered his face to hide his tears from the old man. Tipp gasped for air. Lost in deep anguish, he spun around, kicking a rubber tire. Strangely neat and uniform, nature lined the roadways.

"I see your Lord didn't protect our boats." Mickey gripped the broken oar with both hands and glared at Tipp in disappointment. His voice and his words were almost unrecognizable. He stared frozen like an ancient statue overlooking the broken landscape. "The motor is gone, the stern is busted on that one, a gaping hole in the side of that one." Mickey continued to calculate the destruction.

"I wasn't in the right headspace to see this storm. Not sure what I was expecting, I just knew it would pass us up, turn and wheel to the north Atlantic." Tipp's eyes watered. "I'm sorry."

While Mickey mumbled about the irreparable damage to his fleet, Tipp sat at the edge of the dock by a tire swing rope that had wrapped itself around the trunk of a Sycamore tree. The tide pulled boards loose from the docks and removed older ones from the posts and beams. Sailboats collapsed onto the bank, two boats were half a mile out into the littered marsh, while several of the other battered boats bobbed in the rough waters. A boat Mickey had recently pulled from Charleston to Whitemarsh Island was also missing in action.

"Your prayers didn't work for me, Tipp," Mickey repeated, kicking the nets. "Now what?"

"You mean the prayer hasn't worked yet. Besides, how would you know? God still has a plan for you, Grandpa."

Tipp fully believed what he'd said to the old man. He desperately needed God to work in his grandfather's life and fast. Touching his family name on the side of what was the very first fishing boat Mickey had bought with his own money, he pounded the vessel with his fist. Now it's been discarded by the storm surge-- a multitude of broken pieces are just memories of what the fleet once provided. The old man fell to his knees in the muddy water and was up to his eyeballs in debt. The cost of replacing the fleet would be astronomical and frankly, impossible to recoup. While his lifestyle was certainly affluent, his cash flow was not. He needed cash for his men immediately, and settling with the insurance company could drag on for months, possibly years. He didn't have time to liquidate any assets.

"I know you can't see it now, but something good will happen," said Tipp, kicking a path through the wreckage. "It will happen. I have bigger faith than any storm."

"You're right about that; I definitely can't see it." Mickey rested his hand on the stern of his nearly unidentifiable shipwreck, pounding his latest purchase.

"God will give us double for our trouble." Tipp sleeved his face and wiped the sweat and emotion down with the back of his hand.

"Let's head back home; I've seen enough nautical nightmares." Mickey tried to push one of his boats back into the water. The old man laughed eerily to himself, hoping to ease the pain. "Just take me home," he murmured, kicking a life jacket off the ramp's end.

"We're alive and healthy, aren't we?" Tipp asked, trying to change his tone. "And we're both still devastatingly handsome, huh?"

"I'm dead on the inside." Mickey's face had turned from boiling red to a snowfall pale.

"You have your grandmother's heart," he said, dragging up the ramp, "I'll give you that much."

"Let's stay positive," said Tipp, squeezing his grandfather's shoulder.

"Positive doesn't put fish in my nets or pad my bank account."

"Fire up the truck and let's go." Mickey rolled down the window. The sight of his boats replaced all remnants of the night of binge drinking, sobering his thoughts.

"Looks like the government has sent in more troops since we got here," Tipp stopped the truck.

"Well, wait, hey, look!" His grandfather popped up and rolled the window down. "That's our friend, Hendricks. Let's shoot the breeze with him. Park next to those soldiers." Pointing at a big guy and leaning out the window, "Yep, that's Hendricks," Mickey confirmed.

"Volt Hendricks, the singer, he's back?" Tipp parked, leaning on the steering wheel to see his friend. "We haven't jammed with him in a while."

Mickey formed a bullhorn with his hands. "Volt Hendricks, how are you, my friend?"

"Mickey Starr, how the heck are ya, man?" Volt extended a firm handshake. "I see you two knuckleheads refused to evacuate as the Governor advised."

"Doing fine," said Mickey. "I was much better before this hurricane knocked us down. This is quite the sight, huh?" Mickey rubbed the beads of sweat from his forehead; the wreckage turned his head. "Homes were hit hard."

"It's not good, man," said Volt, surveying the damage. "I hate it. This site is sadder than country music in Nashville." The soldier lightened the somberness with a smile on his face. Then he adjusted his hat and sighed, "Damn hurricane!"

Mickey flipped his hat in his grandson's direction. "Tipp here, says he has faith, says that I'm gonna get double for my trouble," he said, laughing. "Can't wait to cash in on his creative imagination."

Volt chuckled nervously, unsure of how to react. The soldier looked at Tipp. "That's a tall order, but you're a smart college boy."

"Nothing we could have done to save them, I guess." Tipp bit his lip, watching the squad direct traffic and remove trees. "Keep the faith, though."

Leaning on the truck mirror, Volt sympathized, "Hate to hear it, Mick. Just sucks like hell." He took a step back and gazed into the cab of the truck. "Tipp, you still playing that six-string?"

"Every chance I can get," Tipp turned a big smile, loosening his grip on the steering wheel.

"What type of music?" Volt turned to Tipp, happy to change the subject.

"Mostly 60s and 70s rock, some country mixed in."

"We should jam sometime. My leave starts next week. I can hang here for a bit. Let's get together, maybe write some songs, lay down a few tracks. I'll bring down some of my equipment from North Carolina, and we can use my friend's studio in town. Mick, it would be great if you'd join in."

Mickey pulled at his goatee. "Sounds like a plan. You can stay at Tipp's home downtown, so you don't have to trek back so much. But truthfully, the traffic is so dreadful; you're much better off staying at my place. Doors are open, and there's beer," he offered, grinning and lifting one eyebrow.

"Well, now, that's a deal I can't pass up," Volt said, turning his head as two trucks rolled by.

"See you next week," said Mickey, stepping out of the truck to shake hands with Volt and salute properly.

A soldier shouted from a Humvee, "Let's go, Hendricks!"

Volt asked, "What's going on?"

"They caught a man looting boats," reported the soldier. "The police have him in custody, but we are called to work the area, so there's no more looting at the marina." Volt directed his attention to Mickey and Tipp, "Have you folks heard of Carter Cigar and the Bull River Boys?"

The soldier signaled at Volt again. "Your muscles are needed, Hendricks. Get in the back."

"Gotta go, boys, duty calls," said Hendricks before they could answer his question. "I'll catch up with you next week." He slammed the door of the Humvee and was gone.

As their friend rushed off, Mickey sang an old Army cadence, "Everywhere we go. People wanna know. Who we are. So we tell them."

Mickey continued singing, and Tipp joined in to harmonize as the two slowly navigated the truck back down the road. Volt's unit rolled out nearly a dozen trucks between the marina in Whitemarsh Island and the historic district of Savannah. Mickey and Tipp stopped in traffic when the sudden realization of the storm's catastrophic damage meant the old man wasn't the only one who lost everything. Denying his self-pity and thinking about the despair of others, somehow made the pain easier to stomach.

In the background, the two could hear the soldiers working. "Let's get this station set up. Grab that barricade, Jackson. Let's reroute this traffic and get these folks moving," barked the sergeant.

"Got it!" returned Jackson. Gravel crunched as dozens of trucks and end loaders started to open the roads and remove timber. Water and food stations were nearby for returning residents finding themselves without utilities. Volt waved from a distance while holding on to the Humvee.

"Fort Stewart was where I first met him," explained Mickey, as he observed the neighborhood. "We were working on a few songs before units were deployed. I found him to be a humble man. You'd never know he was a real-life rock star, would you?"

"Yep. Great guy," said Tipp, driving slowly. "He became more popular after he joined the Army."

"Yeah, even after having a hit on the radio, he stayed in." Mickey sat up tall, adjusting his seatbelt. "Said he gave his word and made a promise to serve his country. Mickey bragged, "Undeniably selfless man, right there." The old man cracked a smile in admiration.

"He draws a large crowd on military bases, too. A regular modern-day Elvis Presley." Tipp rolled up the windows and turned on the air conditioner. As the traffic crept a little further, he found an opening to make a sharp cut onto the highway.

"Don't chase money or you will miss out on life, the important stuff," Mickey warned him with an air of experience.

"We sure had a good time last year playing gigs; we even did a few songs together," said Tipp. "That guy knows every single song ever written," shaking his head in dismay. "How does he do it?"

"Your old girlfriend, Beth, was around then, too, right?" asked his grandfather. "You still talk to her?" Mickey knew the answer. "You can't keep all the fish you catch, can ya?"

"Not so much these days. That's my fault, though, like a fool, I let her get away." Tipp's voice slowed, checking his rearview mirror as if he could go back and change things. The two grew quiet as the humming of the tires, and the terrain drowned their thoughts. He missed her.

"They'll be another lady soon," Mickey said, grinning. "Have some faith, Doubting Thomas."

Forcing himself to change the subject, Tipp interjected, "I remember the first time I saw Volt on stage. The scene was crazy. Ladies were everywhere. He emerged out of the darkness with a guitar strapped on his back. And when the spotlight hit, the audience went nuts. Screaming girls and bras were on stage before he could finish the first song. One lady rushed the stage and kissed him before security could nab her." Tipp turned down his driveway at Whitemarsh Island. "Absolute insanity."

They both chuckled, and Tipp turned red. "Volt might be able to help you get Beth back," teased Mickey. "Give you a few pointers on women."

Tipp slapped the steering wheel and laughed even harder. "Miracles happen."

"If you ever kept a steady girlfriend, now that would be a damn miracle." Mickey grabbed Tipp's shoulder. "You need to check on your home."

"Umm," Tipp moaned. "I need to make my way to downtown Savannah."

"See Beth, call her while you're in town." Tipp pulled into the bay.

Although Mickey's color hadn't returned to his face, the humor in his words comforted Tipp. "Let's get inside, see if we can figure out a way to get this fleet back up and running again. Lease some boats in Pooler or Charleston," Tipp offered as he patted his grandpa's arm.

Mickey reached for his wallet. "Well, we need to make some money and fast," he stressed, flipping through his wallet.

4

Promises

Mickey's face was the color of a southern biscuit as his thoughts drifted back to the words that Nedra spoke to him before her strength faded. Her sweet voice was soft, yet clear, even in her last days. One night, she grabbed Mickey's hand, and with her eyes full of tears, she whispered, "Please don't worry or feel bad for me. I'll always be with you in your heart. You are the love of my life. I'll visit you in your dreams. I love you, Mickey Starr. Please keep the boats running for Tipp so he can continue the family legacy and one more thing." She cleared her throat and gripped his hand tightly. Mickey leaned in close to her hospital bed. "What is it, honey?"

Nedra pulled one hand loose to cover her cough. "Please try and get my barn back," she pleaded.

Placing her fingertips against his face, Mickey took a deep breath. "For you, I will, dear. Don't you worry about the barn. Get some rest. I love you too." He squeezed her hand once more then kissed her softly on the lips. As Mickey headed toward the door, Nedra realized she could no longer retain her tears. Just before exiting the room, Mickey returned to her. He saw her cheeks were moist with freshly fallen tears, and with a gentle brush of the back of his hand, he removed them from her beautiful face. "Get some rest."

Nedra missed her boy; she wished to have him by her side. Danny's Christian missionary work in the Congo of Africa was the only source of contention between the loving couple. Nedra supported her son's choice to serve the Lord despite it taking him to the African jungle as a Samaritan. Danny had no idea his mother's health was failing. He was nearing the halfway point of his stay. No communication, no contact whatsoever was possible due to the remote and isolated area in which the team had ventured to set up camp. Danny's choice to join the missionary field was sacrificial for them all. Nedra would mask her longing to hug her only child safely in her arms with the pride she felt for Danny's important mission. She funneled her longingness to see him into an extra dose of grandma's love on Tipp. Nedra made it a priority for Tipp not to feel abandoned by Danny's call on his heart to the mission field.

Although Tipp was grown, she didn't want him to feel neglected emotionally or nutritiously.

Her husband, however, felt quite different about the matter. Mickey figured Danny would help him with the business, and now that Nedra was sick, the fisherman was further infuriated. He regretted that Danny couldn't be here with his mother to comfort her, to offer her peace and solace about his well-being mission, in Savannah. Mickey needed his son by his side to help run boats. In his mind, the three men could tag team the duties of the boats while also spending the last precious moments with his beloved wife. Her husband often commented on how there was plenty of mission work to do in Chatham County. In trying to sway Danny's opinion, Mickey would ask, "Why don't you help folks around here?" The difference in opinion drove a wedge between father and son, recognizing the need to no longer speak about Christianity during meals.

Mickey slept as close as he could to Nedra each night. The hospital room was chilly, and the busyness of the nurses offered them little sleep after dark. The soft light in the hall made her think of heaven. Nedra talked and laughed about old times at the barn. Mickey recalled each time Nedra reached for her coffee cup and said, "Cream and sugar, Sugar."

Her bloodshot blue eyes squinted as she caught her breath. She cried and told him how bad she felt. The hospital coffee didn't taste the same as it did at home, and a good cup of coffee was especially important to Nedra. Her taste buds had changed, and her palette was different. Nothing tasted the same as it did at home. Stretching her arm, she reached for Mickey's hand. The cafeteria was as far as he would travel from her room. Once, he visited the chapel, but it didn't impress him much.

"Take me home, can you?" she asked, crying. "To the tobacco barn, I'm packed and ready. I need to go home."

"We will be home soon, dear," he promised, kissing her. "I'll even bring you coffee water from your dad's spring or well if you'd like." He loved her so much; he would have crawled to the well if it would make her better.

"I miss daddy's coffee, don't you?"

Following with a sad smile, Mickey said, "I do, honey, and I miss the trails near the flower fields and the horses in the pasture."

Nedra lifted an empty coffee cup to her lips, and her eyes closed. He noticed she talked to herself when the medication kicked in, sending her into a different world, far, very far from him, sometimes, he thought. Once, she even spoke to her father, Daniel, just as if he stood beside them in the room. Her father died in '74. Her mother, the following spring. Died of a broken heart, Mickey told Nedra after the funeral. But on that particular day, Nedra spoke to her mother and father, having a full conversation about how good the cornbread and beans tasted. Nedra even had Mickey ask her father about unloading trucks in the fall and hanging tobacco in the barn. For hours, she spoke with her parents, and he played along, answering questions and nodding in agreement, but it made her happy. The nurses sympathized with Mickey from the doorway and hugged Nedra when she needed one.

At other times, the couple talked about repairs the barn needed before winter from the last storm, including the doors. Mickey loved to see her smile and tried every way imaginable to make her feel loved. Her gentleness felt like home, and he knew it made her feel good to talk about the tobacco barn and picking fresh-cut wildflowers.

Fridays were extra-special. Mickey would plan hospital date nights with Nedra. Nurse Tara assisted his beautiful bride with her makeup and brushed her thin gray hair. Together, they would help Nedra put on a dress. Although Nedra rarely indulged in lavish materialistic things, a new dress would bring about a certain glow. On the other hand, Mickey had a flair for the finer things, and each time he spoiled her with trinkets and bracelets, she'd welcome the gifts graciously then tuck them away in a homemade felt bag for safekeeping.

On Fridays, Mickey selected a suit then shined his shoes in preparation for his hot date. He'd match his shoes with a black belt, sporting his pocket watch on the left side, and teased Nedra that it was because he didn't want to miss a minute with her. She mentioned how her soldier cleaned up real nice, so he was careful to comb his hair to the side and trim his goatee, like when they first met. Around five o'clock, Mickey rushed back to the hospital for their date with a fragrant bouquet of fresh flowers for her and a spicy cologne she loved on his neck.

The squeaking of the wheelchair bothered Nedra, so he quieted the wheel with oil he brought from his garage. She kissed him for his thoughtfulness. Tonight, the two lovebirds pretended to be at the movies. Afterward, they went for a drive down the hospital hallways and waved at visitors as if they were old friends passing by. She was unusually sprite this evening. It must be a good sign that she's having a good day, Mickey thought.

On warm evenings, Mickey would roll her outside near the birdhouses down past the wooden picnic tables. They often stopped to see the koi pond, where she would talk to the spotted fish and dropped feed into the water. Nedra would squeal with delight when the fish jumped and flapped their tails. Mickey admired her love for nature and appreciated how simple things made her smile most.

Settling into a quiet part of the park, the couple took refuge under a large sugar maple tree where they enjoyed a picnic dinner. The fistful of medicine made Nedra sick on her stomach, and she only pretended to nibble her food. He noticed. Anything she didn't touch, he left for the nurses on the night shift.

Mickey hated seeing his companion suffer and wrestled with the concept of bad things happening to good people. He couldn't understand the purpose of long-suffering and found her illness to be cruel and undeserving. During this time, he'd wonder why the Lord upstairs wouldn't let him take her place and suffer instead. The lack of explanation distanced Mickey even further from her God. One-night Nedra admitted that she didn't want to leave him under any circumstances, not even for the golden streets of glory. Mickey was confused. Was this the medicine talking? The uncertainty haunted him.

While pushing the wheelchair back to the room, Nedra spoke with great honesty, "I saw Him."

Mickey questioned her innocently, "You saw who?"

"The Lord." She reached back for him. Mickey responded by touching her shoulder.

"You mean, you saw God? From Heaven?" The pitch in his voice shot high. "Are you sure?" Mickey was both curious and scared.

Nedra explained further, "He was dressed in a long white robe, standing in a doorway that seemed far too small. And then he did this," Nedra motioned, holding her arms open as if hugging the air, "with His arms."

Mickey struggled to listen to the details as his thoughts whirled inside his head. Without another word, they both knew the inevitable. Mickey hid his tears from his darling as he scooped her frail body and gently placed her back into the bed. He was terrified, but he refused to let Nedra sense it. His focus snapped back to Nedra's voice, saying, "You were with me in a new place."

Mickey lightened the mood by saying, "That's because I'll follow you anywhere." He respected the anticipation Nedra expressed about her vision even though he didn't walk the same spiritual trail as the others. During their marriage, Nedra would often present her case as evidence, and he listened, respectfully; he never agreed, or rebutted. Mickey cared only about being with her and making her feel special, not about their differences. Still, her faith was as strong as forged steel.

"You know we have been together for forty years," she added with a weak voice.

Mickey spoke softly, "I love you more than you will ever know, doll. Could you stay, my love, just a little longer? Please Nedra? I'm not ready." Mickey kissed her forehead.

Nedra opened her tired blue eyes and gazed lovingly at him. She was much stronger than him in many ways. Nedra raised her hand with enough strength to place it on top of his. The sagging hospital wristband made him realize how much weight she'd lost. He had no idea things would advance so abruptly as he stood staring, not knowing what to do or say.

"Take me home, to the tobacco barn. My bags are packed," Nedra pleaded.

"Nedra. Darling. Please stay." Mickey openly sobbed as he lost the need to hide his pain from her.

"Join me someday, will you? Me, you, Danny, and Tipp all together. It will be wonderful. Promise?"

Nedra's eyes shut softly, and her breathing slowed. Mickey toiled over what to do. A call to Tipp was needed, contact her family, but selfishly he stayed by her bedside, holding her hand. Afraid to turn away, he kissed her tenderly on the lips. No response. He knew.

5

Recovery

Mickey wept for weeks that felt like years. Drinking helped pass the time, but he wanted to dull the pain even more by staying in bed. Still, he quenched his thirst for loneliness. More and more and more. He drank because he lost his best friend and the source of everything good in his life, as if the best part of him had died with her, inside and out, his face red in pain. He struggled to maintain his fishing business. Even simple tasks were neglected, creating a snowball effect of late deliveries, missed deadlines, and waves of disappointments. His true love was gone. His zeal for business and life was no longer anchored.

Customers called for orders. Mickey chipped away at generations of good business relationships. In the beginning, many of the customers understood his loss, but soon their patience wore thin, and business tanked. It was tough on Tipp, too. Decades of rapport established with much of the clientele in Savannah and Charleston unraveled. Others didn't take too kindly to dealing with his grandson, Tipp, just some punk kid fresh out of college didn't impress them. Harsh voices haunted Tipp and drove him to dread the fishing business just as much as Mickey did.

Refusal to board his boats and fill the orders fast enough, Mickey lost his spirit to live and work. He was spiraling out of control. Some of his best crew members grew nervous about their future and soon joined the competition. Charles and Ralph sailed with a charter company to Virginia. Bobby caught a bus to New Orleans to work offshore. Max went back to Maine to work on a lobster boat. Without reliable and experienced workers, hard times lay ahead. Rude and nasty messages now filled the fisherman's answering machine, making him feel ashamed of himself.

"Mickey, sorry about your wife, but we need our seafood," said a man with an Italian accent. "Get those boats out to sea and fill your nets. Give me a call, your old friend Stefano." Mickey didn't blame them for being angry. They needed seafood to make money; it was their livelihood on the line, too. Tipp didn't quite understand the severity of Mickey's situation, but he knew something was amiss. He had just graduated from college when he was obligated to join the family business. Tipp probably wasn't built for this level of legendary responsibility; he was more passionate about dating and playing music with his friends, not fishing.

Nedra had passed close to a year before the hurricane destroyed Mickey's fleet, yet he still couldn't shake his overwhelming sorrow. Tipp could tell he was troubled, depressed. Drinking dulled the pain slightly and helped him function. Being drunk kept him from being a recluse. Coffee got him out of bed, and drinking got him through the day.

Tipp was working his tail off. Between cutting up fallen trees to clear roadways, filling orders and running the leased boats, Tipp was putting in 18-20-hour days. Tired and starved, he stopped by the Cotton Tavern and grabbed a dozen crab cakes for supper. Back at Mickey's, he entered the mudroom where they stored raincoats and rubber boots. Exhausted, Tipp unpacked his gear.

His hind parts found a bench, and with his eyes closed, he removed his boots. "I put the chainsaw in the storage building if you need it! Man, I'm tired," Tipp called from the room to Mickey.

"Pssst!" The sound resonated like a freight train in a dark tunnel. Tipp's ears recognized an all too familiar sound reminding him of his fraternity days in Athens. Still curious, he peeked around the mudroom wall and watched Mickey's fingers start to strum his flat-top guitar. His grandson wasn't in the mood. The old man's voice echoed throughout the high ceilings of the grand living space. Tipp witnessed this nonsense habitually from Mickey over the past year. Mickey bounced back and forth between emotional lows and exuberant drunken highs sprinkled with moments of irrational business decisions.

The old man was stretched out on his blue sectional sofa singing Volt Hendricks' song with a black cowboy hat lowered to block sunlight. He belted, *"Let the thunder roll and the lightning strike, let the bullets fly and the heroes fight, And we won't sleep 'til the enemy pays the price."*

The more he sang, the more frustrated Tipp became with his grandfather.

"Not now, old man," shouted Tipp. "Get up."

Ignoring the raving kid, he continued singing and strumming even louder. *"And we won't sleep 'til the enemy pays the price."*

Tipp rubbed his head stressfully. Reaching his breaking point, he mouthed, "You done making a damn mess of your life?"

He didn't respond, causing Tipp's blood to boil further. The old Mickey was a stickler about being wise with his time, and here he was unable to stand up. Deadbeat. Tipp tossed his rubber boots, and the mud ricocheted between the floor and wall. The boy slammed the wooden door to the hall tree and kicked the wastebasket until it splinted. He shuffled toward his grandfather in drenched clothes. Ignoring Tipp, Mickey closed his eyes, playing possum as Tipp stood in front of him muddy, wet, and in need of soap and water. The old man eased open one eye and cocked his head, turning his face upward with a sharp grin. His bloodshot eyes were a clear sign of his condition.

"You're finally home, I see," laughed Mickey. "How was your day, dear?"

Tipp didn't hold back. "You know the worst thing about you?"

"Was I off-key?" rolling his legs off the sofa to stand, Mickey slipped onto the hardwood floor and moaned from a hard drop. "Oh, that hurt," he grunted. "Is my guitar alright?"

Rolling over and laughing into his favorite blue suede pillow, his face partially hidden from Tipp's sight.

"Get up off the damn floor, old man!" Tipp reached for him. Mickey declined his offer. "You really piss me off, you know that?" nudging him. "Now, get up!"

With all his effort, the old man rolled on his back and stared at the ceiling. "I am up," he rubbed his face with both hands. "I'm looking up." Mickey laughed, "Does that count?"

"Not funny, and it doesn't count." Tipp yanked his grandfather's arm. "The worst thing about you is that you talk about being the best, but now you are the worst. Hypocrite." Mickey wobbled into a seated position. "When life threw you a hard day, you just found a bottle and quit. Folded up and quit!"

"No, I didn't. I finish the bottle and started another one." He dropped his head. "Not a quitter." He closed his eyes, laughing, "Now that was funny."

"It's not funny."

Mickey pushed his way to his knees, moaning and grunting, making the best stance he could with the coffee table's help. Tipp saw his inability to stand and muscled him back up to the sofa with both hands.

The old man scanned his prize trophy collection. "Oh man, that eight-point buck is looking at me." He looked through his cracked and bent glasses. "That big elk is laughing at me too. See, they think I'm funny."

"Foolish," said Tipp, walking to the kitchen. "They think you're foolish."

"Grab me a glass of water." Mickey regained some composure and crossed his legs. "O' yeah, I have some important news for you," he said, pointing at his grandson. "Listen, what I'm about to tell you is great news, my boy."

"Are you dying?" he asked out of concern.

Mickey placed the palm of his hand on his forehead, pretending to check his temperature. He felt for the pulse on his neck and with a serious face, said, "I don't think so."

"What then, funny man?" he asked now with a sharp tone.

"What if we have Volt headline a benefit concert to keep the fishermen afloat until the insurance companies settle with the owners." He twisted to see his grandson better. "You are looking at me now, huh?"

"If we promote it for Volt Hendricks, it would be largely profitable for us, too," making his way toward the bar. "We host the show right here in Savannah," he posed, raising his hands and became sober enough to evaluate Tipp's squinted eyes and frown.

"A concert?" handing Mickey a bottle of water. "Large concert, huh? Nah, I'm not sure about the idea."

Mickey staggered over to the fireplace and stood under the mantle. His shoulder was propped up against the Texas sandstone fireplace as he stared out the doorway. "I like it," Mickey said, swaying slightly, tapping his hands on the wooden mantle. "When Volt drove into town, it was a good sign, right?" He snapped his fingers and caught his balance. Slapping his pockets, searching for tobacco to light up, Mickey came up empty. "I've crunched the numbers," said the old man. "This idea will work."

"You think Volt will do it?"

Tipp cocked his head and cleared his throat, observing how Mickey gloated, who shook his head and sighed in deep relief, his message had finally arrived.

Mickey said with confidence, "Let's just say I know someone who can make a suggestion or two over dinner tonight." His face brightened.

"Who?"

"The most beautiful woman in Savannah," said Mickey. "Our girl next door."

Tipp stood and walked over beside Mickey. Pointing out the window to the girl in the neighboring yard, he questioned, "Shasta? Really? You're going to use Shasta to convince Volt to perform a concert for you? That's a pretty outrageous idea-- I think you should stick to fishing," Tipp teased in a non-supporting demeanor.

"I'm not using anyone." Mickey pulled on his goatee. "Have you considered that they might fall for each other?"

"Hmmmmm," Tipp scoffed doubtfully.

Still, Mickey pressed, "They are about the same age, and she's a prize for a good man."

Tipp crossed his arms. "I like your plan for a big concert," leaning against the door; he continued, "I think Volt's the solution!"

"That's because she's like a sister to you, y'all grew up together." Both men were on the same page for once. "A packed concert could get the bank paid fast," said Mickey nodding his head with his arm on Tipp's shoulder. "And it will keep us out of foreclosure."

Mickey walked to the refrigerator with his head down, ashamed of the pending conversation. Dreading the words that were about to unfold, he knew Tipp was going to blow his top, but he needed to be honest with his grandson.

"Wait! What is this talk about getting the bank paid and letters of foreclosure? Are you about to lose this house?" Tipp shouted, taking a seat. "Huh?"

Mickey walked to the kitchen for more water. Tipp followed.

"Bank wants their money, and I don't have it without boats, my boats."

"What do you mean you don't have it?" Tipp continued questioning in disbelief.

"I don't have it," Mickey's voice raised, "Plain and simple, I do not have the funds to continue paying for all of this stuff," he admitted as he slapped his hands on the bar top.

"How much time do we have?" Tipp asked as he joined Mickey at the bar.

"Sixty days tops."

"How much money?"

Mickey chugged his water to keep from answering questions.

"How much?" Tipp leaned toward his grandfather.

"A lot." Mickey dodged a tough question.

"One more time, old man, how much?" While his voice shook in anger, his tone meant business.

Mickey took a deep breath, and with hesitance, he admitted, "With boat payments, mortgage, and cars..." Mickey turned his body away from Tipp.

"This is the last time I'm going to ask how much money you need?" His grandson gripped his forehead and closed his eyes like he had a migraine. "What the hell have you been doing with all the checks?"

"It goes so fast." The old man paced around the room then stopped to stare outside, avoiding eye contact with his grandson.

"What do you mean it goes fast!" Tipp spun his barstool around and watched Mickey. "What's it going to take for you to learn, huh?"

"Went a little overboard, I guess with cars and a few things."

Tipp scolded him. "Stop buying damn classic cars; you don't need all of this shit."

"I'm accustomed to a certain kind of lifestyle," Mickey answered, brushing his chest with his hand and adjusting his gold watch.

"Well, now you're broke and stuck with a bunch of crap you can't afford." Tipp poured soda.

Mickey turned to look at Tipp. With a cocky smile, he admitted, "I have certain people who expect the Son of the South to live like royalty. And, the truth is, I like it too."

"We have two months!" Tipp moved in closer. His grandfather remembered his drill sergeant from the Army stood that close to him; he despised it. The two men stood nose to nose for the first time. They were matched up like two prize fighters, sizing each other up. Neither of them knew what to say or do next. Mickey was dressed in cowboy boots and denim, while Tipp was half-naked in shorts and wet socks. Their differences were numerous at times.

Tilting his head Mickey kept talking, "Don't worry, Tipp. I took care of your tuition when your dad was in South Africa. Four years later, the fishing business is suffering. You don't want to help your grandfather, who needs you to build the Starr family business up again, college boy?"

"Too late, I'm in, and I've always supported the Starr name. I don't get drunk."

He bucked against Mickey's chest with his grievances about how he treated his legacy and business. On one hand, he appreciated the lifestyle that was handed to him, but Tipp felt blocked from his own dreams, suppressing his anger for too long. Being the one always to take the high road and just like his wonderful grandmother, he was quick to smooth things over when he spotted a mess. Like her, Tipp would rather be wrong than be at odds, well, most of the time. Mickey was proud he was ready to fight and took a stand. On occasion, a rare occasion, Tipp would lash out with his grandpa's quick temper. Often, Tipp hugged his grandpa to stifle the tension between them. A drunken Mickey misread his motive and pushed him back against the refrigerator.

"Fire away, big boy." Mickey chuckled as Tipp grabbed his arm, catching him off guard. He spun his grandpa around, wrapping Mickey up and forcing him to the cold hard tile floor.

"You're drunk, and I'm pissed," said Tipp, who had him locked. "But we're not going to swing it out, old man. Now, get up and let's talk this out. Tipp turned Mickey on his side and pulled him up to a stable position. "Why don't you sell the cars or the Hilton Head cottages and keep the mansion?"

"Tipp, a man can't break up a good car collection now, can he?" joked Mickey.

He explained to Tipp that liquidation would not be quick enough to be worthwhile, but inside, Mickey struggled at the thought of parting with his prized possessions. He wanted his remaining crew to continue providing for their families, and felt a sense of responsibility in ensuring it happened. However, he was proud of what he owned and viewed parting with them as a sense of failure, at worst, public humiliation, and the newspapers would hit him from all sides.

Mickey stroked his goatee and found his broken glasses under the cabinet. "I see your point, fisherman."

Tipp looked at him. "Good. I'm glad you do, Captain Starr," he said. "I'm glad you do. Here's your water. Drink it and sober up."

Mickey grinned at Tipp.

"With a little soap and the water hose, see if you can clean that dead alligator and rotten fish smell off your ass?" teased Mickey.

Tipp picked up the barstool they'd knocked over and tidied up the kitchen.

"I didn't hurt you, did I?" Mickey asked, laughing and drinking his water.

Tipp hugged his grandfather tight. Some things just aren't worth the battle, he thought.

Mickey opened Tipp another can of soda, "Here's an appetizer." They laughed.

"Speaking of appetizers, where's Raquel?" His grandson opened the door to a small food prep room.

After a few minutes of waiting, Mickey walked back to the kitchen, checked the storeroom, and called for her, finding her note about being at the store.

"We'll need a special dinner for our guests tonight," said Mickey. "Raquel is one rare lady." He bragged about Raquel's cooking and how they'd become good friends.

"You need to sober up and enjoy the night," warned Tipp. "Be a good host to your guests. I have to run to Savannah and get ready. What time will Volt and our neighbor friend get here?"

Mickey followed Tipp into the great room. "We'll chat a while and see what happens." The host pressed his hands together like a magician.

"Sounds like you've thought this thing out." Tipp sat down in front of the fireplace.

"I have." Mickey nodded and adjusted his cowboy hat and collar.

Tipp grinned, saying, "But will it work... Tex?"

"We'll see, Tippie," Mickey replied, letting go of his collar.

"Surround yourself with good friends and see what happens." Mickey toasted Tipp with an imaginary glass of champagne.

"We'll see," replied Tipp, raising his eyebrows. While Tipp polished off a crab cake, Mickey stood in the living room and watched the beautiful sunset. He was deep in thought, thinking of Nedra, maybe also ashamed of his behavior toward his grandson. Perhaps, he was thinking of a backup plan if Volt wasn't interested. Before long, the sun dropped out of the sky.

6

Three Beers and One Prosecco

Hundreds of guests had visited Mickey's palatial home in Whitemarsh Island, Georgia. Live music and catered events were spoken of for months. Lights hung from the Texas longhorns mounted above the fireplace and wrapped around the banisters that led guests to the second level. A radiant long-haired French chef, named Raquel was ready to add a culinary twist to the night.

His custom-made wine cellar could make a sommelier blush. His home stored wooden cases of the best port known in the states. Paris was his favorite city, outside Savannah, and his quarter-turned kosher oak barrels were once on vines in Loire, France, shipped to him the season prior. He planned to show Volt the newest additions to his classic car collection. The old man felt amiss inside, he needed money, but no one would know it to look at him. He never bragged about what he had, he genuinely enjoyed sharing his good fortune with others. He made sure each guest felt catered to, honing his knack for making others feel special, it was his way of thanking them for their friendship.

Dressed in his favorite imported sport coat, Mickey chose a white oxford shirt and baby blue necktie. His spirit had heightened because he'd planned to play matchmaker and hoped it would reveal grand results. Shasta was the neighbor's daughter, and being Tipp's age, the two practically grew up together. The duo would climb trees, watch movies, and swim all summer long. Shasta was beauty and brains combined. Mickey often loaned convertibles to her father for Shasta to sit atop in parades. Currently home visiting her parents from traveling for multiple modeling gigs made his plan perfect. Underneath the glitz and glam, Shasta was a regular girl. Tipp used to say she was tall and sassy and a little smart-assy, but she hadn't let fame remove her humility.

Mickey was a thinker who mulled ideas over in his head. Nedra would say that he was the dreamer, and she was the realist. Together they were the perfect match for business and marriage. He missed her so much.

The host saw his guest arrive from the second-floor window. Volt looked unsure and wondered if he was the only guest invited to the Starr home on that evening.

"George is running a few errands, he'll be back shortly to help," Mickey called down to Tipp. "So, could you greet our guest, please?"

The doorbell rang. "I got it." Tipp hollered, walking toward the entrance, opening the door, "Come on in, Volt! Welcome back to Mickey's humble abode."

"A good soldier is always early for his mission," commented Volt. "On time is ten minutes too late in the military." The two snickered while shaking hands in an overly masculine manner.

"Good to see you, man," said Volt, stepping inside the grand scale living room. "This isn't a meager homestead by any means, it's quite a grand palace of a place."

Tipp humbly acknowledged his comment as Volt walked through the grand foyer. "Make yourself at home. I'll check on Mickey." Tipp ran up the stairs to see what was keeping him. Meanwhile, Volt wandered around the great room, feeling the elaborate stonework of the fireplace with his bare hands and admiring the wildlife mounts on the walls. Tipp returned promptly.

"Mickey keeps good beer on hand, like one while we wait?" Tipp motioned for Volt to follow him in the next room.

"Yes, sir, you know I do." He found a seat at the bar not far from the door.

Tipp held up two beers, "Domestic or imported?"

"I'm not picky about brew, something from the Rockies, a long neck if you got it." Volt took the icy chilled bottle that Tipp handed him. "Mickey busy?" he asked.

"He'll be down in a minute. The old man is always primping his hair and goatee." Volt placed his beer on a coaster from Buffalo

Joe's Bar & Pub, gazing at one of Mickey's *Best in Show* horse trophies from Lexington, Kentucky.

"You gotta look nice for the ladies," bragged Mickey as he entered the room. "How's the Army treating you, Volt?"

Volt pulled on his tie. "Not too bad, I guess, at least not yet. The defense department has developed some new equipment they want to test in the sandbox. So, they've deployed a few thousand soldiers to Bosnia and other places to help with that," he exhaled with some uncertainty. "I might have to go soon."

Tipp pulled up a chair beside their guest. "Not good, is it? Bosnia, Iran, Iraq, are the hot zones right now, right?"

Volt's eyes blinked as he shook his head.

"Rice paddies. Jungles. Sandboxes. It's bad news for soldiers," he shared solemnly and took a swig of his beer. "Got buddies already over there."

Tipp sipped his soda. "We don't need another damn oil war or 444 days of hostages."

Volt pointed to his bottle. "Gonna have to run this beer off in the morning. Trying to stay in shape for the stage, not the Army." The duo laughed hard.

"Let's do five at five, if you're up for it, that is."

"Five miles at five o'clock?" Volt nodded in agreement and flexed his arm.

"George prepared your room." Tipp pointed down the hall. "He'll grab your luggage when he returns."

A liking man entered the room and rushed to shake Volt's hand. "Nice to see you again, Mr. Hendricks. I've heard your new song on the radio," turning a big smile on his chiseled face. "The newspaper predicted a number one hit again."

"George..." said Mickey, standing amid the men, "When you have a moment, could you get Volt's things to his room, it may rain?"

"Glad someone is listening to my songs."

"My family are huge fans," said George. "Yeah, Mickey, and it sure is nice to know a real star," George left the room, bent over laughing and clapping his hands.

Volt finished his beer. "It must be nice being called, sir, and not be in the service." Volt waved for another one. "Thanks for the brew, Tipp," he said when Tipp slid the bottle down the bar.

"George has worked here for years. Tipp wasn't as big as boxer pup when he moved to Whitemarsh Island," Mickey told the singer. "Don't know what I'd do without him. Nedra adored him, too." Mickey stared at a picture of Nedra in her youth.

Lightening the mood, Tipp said, "Make yourself at home. Mickey's barracks are yours for as long as you need. Take advantage of his lavish lifestyle, Grandpa doesn't cut corners with guests." Tipp tugged at his sport coat and poured the two men a shot from the bar.

Volt felt the warmth from the drink. "Hey, I could get used to this high life." He choked back the strong drink. "I should have gone into fishing instead of joining the Army," kidded Volt.

"I'm pretty sure you're raking it in on stage," teased Mickey. "Bills, bras, broads, what more could a man want?" Mickey raised his shot glass to initiate cheers; Volt followed suit. Tipp settled for a tall glass of sweet tea.

"Not like this home," said Volt. "Did everything work out with the insurance and your fleet being wrecked by the storm?" Volt asked, leaning forward. "Got a backup plan in place?"

Tipp's eyes widened. He looked at Mickey, dreading the upcoming conversation about asking Volt for help with a concert. Tipp took a deep breath waiting for Mickey to lower the boom, leaning back with an open mind.

Weighing his options of bringing up the topic so early in the night, Mickey said, "Look at you and your label, though, congratulations on your record deal." Mickey grabbed himself another beer. "Must be tough working for Uncle Sammy and selling tickets on the side." He decided to wait for a better time to ask the singer. "The key is having the right connections and knowing the right people who can spread your name across the marketplace and with the media."

"Grandpa knows all about getting your name out there." Tipp leaned in, gulping his tea. "The Starr Fishing Company is plastered all over Savannah, far beyond Charleston, and even the Outer Banks buys our brand."

"You're welcome," Mickey joked, the man turned and stood to his guest. "You are a gear head, right, Volt?

"Yeah."

"Well, let me show you my newest babies."

Volt clutched his drink. "I'd love to see what's new in your museum."

Mickey motioned for the men to join him.

Opening the doors and turning on the lights, Volt was taken aback. "Outstanding collection, just takes my breath away. Makes me feel like writing a few more songs. Man, Mickey, you know how to get a man jealous."

"I don't know how he finds cars like this," said Tipp, pacing behind them.

Mickey waved his hand again. "I didn't have this one last year." That dark blue '66 Corvette in the corner and the burgundy '34

Vickie are new. Hard to believe they were both covered in cobwebs and pigeon crap when I found them, huh?"

Walking behind Mickey nervously, Volt made sure not to stumble onto the relics. He paused and soaked it all in. "Unbelievable! Mickey, this is the most cars I've ever seen in a private collection." Jamming his hand into his pocket, he examined the glossy red and black paint of a '68 RS Camaro. Reaching through the downed window Volt gripped the steering wheel and observed a flawless restoration. The singer carefully opened the door and slid slowly down in the seat, pounding went on inside his chest, and his heart skipped a beat. Reaching down, he pulled the hood latch and crawled out to see the engine with Mickey's approval. "If you ever get the courage to let me drive one of these, just hand over the keys, I'll take you up on it."

"Well, you never know when I might need a favor, maybe we can take it out in trade," Mickey hinted and nodded at Tipp.

Unfortunately, unloading a car or two from the collection would not salvage the fishing business, and there's no way the bank would give him enough time to liquidate. Deep down, he was relieved.

"How many cars in total?" Volt looked across the room at an array of colors, a palette any artist would be excited to muse. "I counted 36."

"His classic black truck is in bay three," said Tipp.

"I have 49 cars in all, but only 37 are here, the rest are in Atlanta," Mickey answered, heading toward the light switches. "I'm looking for that special one, though, a pick of the litter type, so to speak. That will make my collection hit 50."

Volt nodded. "Do you mind if I crank up this black Phantom?"

"That's a '31 Rolls Royce Phantom," added Tipp. "The car replaced the Silver Ghost. Mickey traded a Kentucky Thoroughbred for that car."

"I'll have to find the keys to the '31, in the meantime, crank the Rally Sport Camaro, the keys are in it, start it up." Mickey stepped back and supported his words with a thumbs up.

"I will drive this baby in the morning if that's alright?" said Volt, gripping the wheel again. "I want to be careful, I mean, I'd like to open it up and shake it." They laughed.

"Tipp will open the bay for you whenever," said Mickey as he handed Tipp the keys.

"Why are you taking the time to show me all this stuff?" asked the soldier.

"There's an old Irish saying, 'A good friend is like a four-leaf clover; hard to find and lucky to have.' Tipp and I feel honored to know you. Nedra would too," said Mickey. "You saw pictures of my wife, right?"

"Yeah, of course. Heck of a woman, what a fighter. I'm so sorry for your loss. I know how tough that must have been."

"It's been a long year," said Mickey. "We needed a change of scenery to take our minds off our loss, the storm, life in general, I guess." Mickey unbuttoned his sports coat.

"Well, I'm not going to be your wife if that's what you're thinking," teased Volt. "We're not that good of friends."

Mickey belted out a cackle that echoed throughout the gallery. He slapped the soldier's shoulder. "You're quite the entertainment, I like that about you, Volt."

"He can sing and has a sense of humor." Tipp leaned against the wall and flashed a friendly smile.

Mickey rubbed his stomach. "I don't know about you, gentlemen, but I'm somewhat hungry. What time is it, Tipp?"

"Dinner time," Tipp swiftly replied.

"Good! That's my favorite time of the day." Mickey excused himself and hurried down the corridor to greet the next guest arriving.

"Where's he going so fast?" Volt asked, raising his eyebrows.

"Back to the bar probably," Tipp added sarcastically.

"I like good beer and good food, myself," said Volt. "You lead the way."

"Are you expecting anyone else?" asked Volt, making small talk as they walked back to the living quarters.

"Yeah, warning, grandpa's trying to play matchmaker with you and the neighbor."

Volt adjusted his tie, brushed his hand through his short hair, and flattened his sport coat.

"Is she nice and by nice, of course," clearing his throat, "I mean, hot as the Arizona sun?"

"She's a nice girl, alright."

Tipp led his guest past the dining room table. "Let's grab a seat while Mickey brings in our other guest."

George stepped behind the bar area, holding up two glasses, and asked, "What can I get you to drink?"

"Another beer will work for me, please," Volt said eagerly.

"George, bring Mickey a porter, will ya?" asked Tipp. "I'll take flat water with lemon if you don't mind. Thanks, George."

George looked up from opening bottles and greeted Mickey and Shasta when they entered the room.

"Hey, there's my favorite neighbor." Shasta leaned across the bar to hug George.

"You look stunning as always, Miss Shasta," George stated sweetly. "And what is the lady's desire tonight?"

"She likes Prosecco, George," Mickey replied.

Turning towards Volt, she said, "Nice to meet you; I'm Shasta, the next-door neighbor, and I'm a southern belle, so I hug my friends." Shasta gently pushed aside Volt's hand and wrapped her arms around him.

Stunned by her forwardness, Volt responded, "Oh, yeah, hey, I'm Volt, Volt Hendricks."

Tipp pretended to choke on his beer and said, "She's southern, but I wouldn't say, southern belle." Shasta turned to punch Tipp in the arm as payback for the snide remark.

Mickey broke the two apart. "Don't pay him any mind, Shasta. That's why he's still single."

Mickey pulled a cigar from the humidor and signaled for the group to grab their drinks and head out to the patio. "It's a glorious night, isn't it?" Mickey gazed at the dark sky. "The stars are bright, and the river is smooth." He clasped his hands together and sat back in his chair, admiring the view.

Volt couldn't take his eyes off Shasta's black fitted dress and high heels. Her matching bracelet and earrings sparkled in the moonlight. Nervous now, he wished he didn't know Mickey was trying to set him up. Feeling awkward, Volt wondered if Shasta knew about it.

Shasta initiated the conversation, "So, Volt, Volt Hendricks, how do you know this motley crew?"

"I'm good friends with Mickey and Tipp, we played some together last year."

"So, what about you?" asked Volt. "I mean other than location."

"I grew up with Tipp and Mickey, the old man is like a grandfather to me."

Mickey interrupted, "She meant to say that I'm like a brother to her."

The group laughed. Volt shared with Shasta he was in service and played in a band, while Shasta divulged she was a model. Being in two different industries and always traveling, the two didn't realize how accomplished one another was. Mickey spied on Volt, tugging at his collar and flexing his arms. Volt's behavior amused him, and he cracked a smile.

"It's nice to be back home," Shasta sighed. "I haven't seen you two since Nedra's funeral." She hugged Mickey with wide-open arms. "Ms. Nedra was a sweetheart. I miss her, she was like a grandmother to me. I mean, like a sister to me, right, Mickey?"

"Ha! Yes, that's right. She was something else. Broke the mold when they made her," Mickey reminisced while turning his wedding ring around his finger. "We all miss her."

Mickey felt emotionally drained as he imagined Nedra seated beside him on her last Thanksgiving dinner. He fought daily to shake his loneliness, and times like this made him feel somewhat better, even if it was temporary. "Now that we are hungry let's see what Raquel has prepared." The group clutched their beverages and headed to the dining room.

As they were seated, Raquel came to greet the guests. In a thick French accent, Raquel said, "Good evening, everyone. My name is Chef Raquel, and tonight you will begin with a fresh cobb salad. Then for your entree, you will have mouthwatering prime rib from Mickey's ranch in Amarillo and fresh Maine lobster with a perfectly seasoned vegetable medley. And for dessert, a homemade key lime pie topped with creme fraiche. I hope everyone is hungry." As Raquel walked back to the kitchen, George put on some smooth jazz and softly dimmed the lights.

"All my favorite dishes, Mickey," Shasta excitedly replied, unrolling her utensils. "How did you know? Are you a spy?"

"Nope, just observant." Mickey leaned closer to the table. "You have been eating at my house since you were in pigtails-- not long after you moved here from Charleston."

She giggled and sipped her beverage. Mickey witnessed Shasta often glancing out of the corner of her eye at Volt's side of the table. She adjusted the thin black spaghetti strap that fell off her left shoulder, turning Volt's eyes in her direction. Hoping he'd done the right thing by having them over for dinner, Mickey figured his match-making plan was worth a shot, a smart idea that crossed his mind.

While Mickey and Volt talked about musical instruments, he watched how Shasta was consumed by Volt's every move. Sweat beaded up on Volt's forehead as George chuckled, gifting the soldier with a cup of cold ice, whispering low in his ear, "Like the Arizona sun."

When Volt stood to remove his sport coat, Shasta snagged a second glimpse of his tight body. George grabbed Volt's jacket when he returned from with extra ice. His shirt was snug, outlining his chest and tanned neckline. After Volt returned to his seat, Shasta winded his cologne as George took his jacket to the cloakroom. She pushed her chair back from the table.

"Let me get your chair," said Volt.

Shasta moved from the table. "Thanks. I'll be back in a moment. Don't you guys start without me."

Mickey noticed how she turned to look back at Volt as he watched her walk down the hall. The lady giggled on her way to the bathroom. While there, Shasta ran her fingers through her hair and made sure her diamond earrings were snug. After applying a hint of lipstick, she twisted her hips and tugged on her dress to adjust it. Getting final approval from the oval full-length mirror, Shasta sauntered her way back to the dining room to find that George had folded her napkin and placed it neatly on the table.

"I'm back. Hope I didn't keep you gentlemen waiting too long, I'm starving."

"The first course is ready," replied Mickey as he helped with her chair.

Tipp broke the few seconds of silence, "Volt's staying with us a few weeks; gonna practice a few songs and hang out with us guys at Whitemarsh Island."

Mickey tilted his head and waited for her next words to see if any chemistry existed between his guests.

"I could show you around town, that is, if you don't already have a tour guide," Shasta impulsively added. "My schedule is clear until the Thanksgiving Parade in New York."

Volt eyed her and smiled, "Sure, I'd love a tour."

Tipp added, "But you already know..."

Mickey cut him off with his hand and finished the sentence for him, "You already know how to bait a hook, so fishing would be fun."

Mickey passed Shasta the butter dish as George brought fresh bread to the table.

"That sounds like a great idea." Volt cleaned breadcrumbs from the corners of his mouth. "I love to fish."

Months had passed since Mickey had experienced excitement and fun in his own home. His heart was pleased as he sat listening to the others banter about places to go and throwing a line in the water. Bringing people together gave Mickey a sense of satisfaction and a refreshing change of atmosphere compared to the bickering back and forth between the insurance company and the unexpected bout with his grandson. He felt lucky to be among good friends again.

"Tipp, you're joining us, right?" Shasta asked. "You can bring a guest, I mean, girlfriend," teasing him.

"You'll meet her later," Tipp defended himself. "Don't want you fools running her off without me."

"Much later," mumbled Mickey.

The group howled at his reply, and the host had a new glow about him, feeling at peace while watching what he'd brought together unfold. Volt shifted his body toward his new friend Shasta. They whispered back and forth during the meal. Shasta's laugh was contagious and entertained everyone. Mickey wasn't surprised about the positive energy she brought to his house. Educated, hard-working, and fun to be around. The coup de gras was that she was also stunning and financially stable. Mickey didn't want to ruin the mood of the evening by talking business with Volt and doubted he could pull Volt away from Shasta, anyway. Tipp noticed that Mickey had derailed from the plan to speak with Volt about hosting a concert and was unsure why. Shasta finished her wine. George swooped in and refilled her stemware with more Prosecco.

Mickey filled his drink and stood beside George. Tipp eyed Mickey to see if he noticed what was happening at the table. He was alerted to the fact that Volt's hand now rested on her leg. Volt moved his hand down to touch Shasta's bare skin at the bend in her knee. Shasta turned to drink her wine but kept one hand under the table on top of his.

As George cleared the table, Mickey asked, "How about some coffee? Anyone for coffee and dessert?"

"We have fresh ground Colombian coffee, and for Tipp, milk and cookies," announced the butler.

"That was one time when I was ten." Tipp exclaimed, "Geez Louise, I'm never going to live that snack down. Volt, I asked for milk and cookies in the fifth grade. I'm still getting rapid-fire, yet, twelve years later."

Barely able to speak from laughing at Tipp and George, Mickey interrupted the guests as Raquel entered the room, "Excusez-Moi, Raquel." Mickey paused for the group to focus on his chef. "Wonderful dinner, Raquel, Ce repas était vraiment excellent." Mickey's French was sparse, but he tried. "Let's give her a round of applause."

"Merci, Mickey, C'est très sympa de ta part," responded Raquel as she served key lime pie. George poured delicious coffee from a steamy French press. In her signature accent, Raquel uttered in English, "Enjoy everyone." Turning to Mickey, Raquel added, "I'm heading out now, see you at lunchtime tomorrow? Oui?"

"Wow! You're going to be out until lunch tomorrow? Must be some hot date!" Tipp kidded Raquel.

"Oh, Tipp, you and your jokes," said Raquel. "I'd never give a man that much of my time, all American men want to do is show you their..."

George interrupted. "Cocktail anyone?" He waited on his turn to add impeccable comedy to the hour. The room roared with laughter. Raquel even held on to the back of a chair to steady herself while belly laughing.

"I think I should go now, this party is getting out of control, and I don't want to be deported if the police get involved." Raquel teased, then waved goodbye to the group.

The guests finished their pie, and Mickey excused himself from the table. "Tipp and I will be in the game room if you two would like to join us for some pool. Rack 'em up, Tipp, best of three." Mickey took his position in the doorway of his game room.

Tipp leaned in close to Mickey, "Did you forget to ask Volt?" He reminded his grandfather as he racked. "We need his help."

"I know it, Tipp." Mickey knew that asking Volt to play a concert would be profitable, but his pride and unwillingness to ask for help kept him silent. An overwhelming sense of embarrassment caused him to hold his tongue. Mickey worried about asking Volt for financial help with the massive assets he could loosen to remedy the situation. "Timing, Tipp. It's all in the timing," he lectured as he broke the set.

Tipp and Mickey continued playing while Shasta and Volt stayed behind and walked to the outdoor patio. Now alone with Shasta, Volt uncapped a question, "Are you dating anyone?" He leaned against the rock wall and flexed his muscles, unsure of what to expect from her. His eyes trailed her thin silhouette.

Shasta propped her hand on his shoulder. Closer than they'd been all night, she spoke with a stern, businesslike voice. "No," she smiled, "I am not dating anyone."

Volt stood tall and ran his finger slowly under the strap of her dress, lowering it as he grazed at her bronze skin. Her thin frame was feeling the effects of the Prosecco. Shasta pulled her hair to the side, exposing her smooth, yet sun kissed neckline down to her front.

"Since you are not dating anyone, would you like to hang out?" Volt opened the top few buttons on his shirt. The humidity was thick and muggy near the river. He leaned forward on the railing, waiting for her response. His body was firm, attractive and rugged.

George returned with a platter of fruit and more drinks.

"Mickey's request, Sir."

"Thank you, George," Shasta said as she grabbed a glass. Standing under the lamp above the pool, she slipped off her shoes. She slid down the railing to the step and dipped her feet in the pool. The water felt cool and refreshing.

Wiggling her toes in the pool, Shasta lifted her leg across the top of the water more than once as Volt waited on his reply. She twisted around the railing to see if he was watching her make waves, and he moved beside her because of it. Maybe to protect her if she slipped. Pretending to be coy, Shasta sensed there was chemistry between them when he winked at her.

"You have your guard up, I see."

Moving in close enough to kiss her, he said, "I'm sorry the last bastard hurt you, but I'm not him. My father taught me better than that."

"No," shaking her head. "I'm an open book, a simple, plain-Jane Girl Scout from Savannah." She placed her hand over her heart.

"You don't need to oversell it, Sister Catherine," he laughed. "I just got here, see if we can get to know each other first."

She looked up at him. "I'm not selling anything, and I'm not giving it away, either." She stood inches away from his chest and arms.

Volt leaned in for a kiss, and she pulled away. Standing inside the pool, she slipped, but he grabbed her arm, saying, "I got you from here on out."

Relieved she wasn't swimming in the pool. "Didn't you date...?"

"I've dated a lot of nice ladies."

Shasta was angered by his response to her. "What?" she locked her eyes on him. "It's no secret, but it is a major turn off. I was so close to kissing you! You messed up, Volt Hendricks!" She stomped her feet, leaving the pool and walked toward the house. Curling a grin, Volt admired her fit profile in the black dress.

Tipp heard her loud voice echoing across the pool and checked on them.

"Is everything alright? Do you need anything?"

"No thanks, Tipp, it's all good," replied Volt.

Shasta gave him the cold shoulder, but Volt never turned from her soft, hazel brown eyes. She didn't go far, he noticed. Mickey and George joined Tipp on the patio by the pool.

"I'll take another one, George." Volt waved his hand above his head.

Shasta walked over near Tipp and scanned the platter of fresh fruit. Snagging a strawberry, she seductively bit into the fruit. "I'm about ready to leave," she announced, with her intention turned toward Volt.

"You better get going then," Volt turned and said, puckering his lips at her. "You don't want to leave loneliness waiting."

Rendered speechless, Shasta walked past Volt on her way to the house. Stumbling on uneven patio stones, she lost her balance and fell. Accidentally, wine splashed on Volt as she reached for him to break her fall.

"Oh, no!" Shasta looked up at him, thankfully she wasn't hurt. "I am so sorry. I didn't mean to spill red wine on you. Your shirt is ruined." She was immediately embarrassed by her behavior.

Lifting her chin with his hand, she continued to brush wine from his shirt. "Shasta, Shasta, leave it." He tilted her head to see her cherry lips. "I'm fine, please. It's just a shirt," he assured her.

Shasta followed him into the house as he removed the shirt and soaked it in some mineral spirits. Instead, she snatched a kitchen towel from George's station, and vigorously attempted to dry the stain. Volt took the towel and pulled her against him. She pressed in closer, and their lips touched softly. He slid his hands down her side and pulled her hips close toward him. Her hands rested comfortably on his chest. In a considerate gesture, he tucked a strand of her brown hair behind her ear. More relaxed than she'd felt in a long time, she leaned in for a second kiss.

Before it went too far, she stepped back from Volt, drying her lips with her finger. She walked back onto the patio to thank Mickey and hugged Tipp and George as well. "Hey, Mickey, thanks for the great evening. I'm gonna head home now." Her soft smile appeared to Mickey as if she was fond of her newfound friend.

"I'll walk her home," offered Volt. "Make sure the wolves don't get her," he laughed. "I heard this neighborhood was a rough and tough one."

Everyone laughed at his joke. George collected her things. "Your sweater and bag, Miss Shasta," handing her the items. "And your heels."

"Oh, Mickey, one last thing, I'm directing a pageant on Saturday, do you think I could sneak over to the barn and cut some wildflowers from the field?"

The old man's mind faded back to when Nedra picked a handful of flowers from the field.

"I won't tell if you won't," he kidded her.

"Good night, gentlemen," said Shasta.

Once in private, halfway down the sidewalk, she dropped her sweater, shoes and purse beside her bare feet. Volt noticed what she was doing and stopped to watch her. She halted and immediately turned around, kissing him beneath the golden lamppost.

George, Tipp, and Mickey watched them kiss. Ribbing their friend, they called out mocking a ladies' voice, "Goodnight, Volt, Volt Hendricks. Hee, hee, hee." The three amigos waved and snickered. "Goodnight, Shasta, Shasta McGregor!"

They stepped back inside the house and Mickey reminisced about the evening.

"Well, grandson, thank you for the nice distraction from all of the craziness, I'm feeling a little ill. Gonna head on up, now."

"Are you just mad because I finally beat you at a game of billiards?" Tipp teased him.

"I'm sorry, Tipp, did you say something?" Mickey asked, ignoring his victory. Tipp turned back to the window and continued watching the couple. Mickey slowly traversed the stairs leading to his bedroom. Partially up the stairs, he stopped to catch his breath, then continued his journey, pulling himself along, using the handrail. He went straight to bed without undressing.

The couple made it to Shasta's door, and Volt wrapped his hands around her waist. "Glad Mickey was kind enough to pair us together at the table," said Volt.

"He's a wise man," said Shasta. "I'll see you in the morning, at eight o'clock, alright? My dad's up, so I better get inside unless you want to meet him and talk all night."

Volt backed away slowly, pretending to sneak away. She blew him a kiss and rushed inside.

"Who's the new guy?" asked her father.

"Volt."

"There is only one person named Volt," he turned. "Was that Volt Hendricks?" Mr. McGregor walked from his office to the stairs leaning up against her room. "The singer? The soldier with the good voice, that guy?"

"I'm starting to like him on the radio," she told herself. The moon widened brightly through the window. She whispered, "The idea of dating Volt Hendricks is broadening my imagination." She closed her eyes and fell on the bed.

7

Tobacco Road

Daniel and Annie thought that life for most of the world moved too fast. More time needed to be spent in old wooden rockers, catching up with each other on wrap-around porches, like the one he just finished at the Randolph's two-story farmhouse. It felt warm and cozy as he held hands with Annie. To Daniel, a blessed day was when he shared sweet tea, a jar of kosher pickles, and peach cobbler with Annie and Nedra.

The lightly traveled roadway was a forgotten route. Folks with out of state tags occasionally got lost on the dead-end road, looking for an outlet to the main highway. What travelers remembered most about the road was the attractive landscape, lush flower fields, tall barns, horses, and endless fences. Being the first residents, the Randolph's referred to the area as Tobacco Road, the name stuck.

From the '40s until the late '60s, Tobacco Road was a tight turnaround for tractor-trailers delivering tobacco from Connecticut and North Carolina. The barn itself was made famous through pictures, postcards, and even an unexplained visit from a filmmaker, the year Kennedy was shot. Nedra's father, Daniel took two years to build the grand structure, a hundred-and-twenty-feet long, ninety-five-feet wide and forty-one feet tall. The completion was a happy one for the Randolphs. When a passerby stopped for pictures of the large red barn, Daniel would stop working and talk to the folks. At times, he even toured them around the property if he wasn't busy cutting tobacco. He was proud of what he had built for his family and thrilled that others were interested in seeing it.

Photographers enjoyed visiting the area for the beautiful gray moss curtained against the high trees. The barrel sized oaks delighted their lenses and made people feel like they were stepping straight into a fairy tale. Pinto ponies stood alongside the narrow pathways near the half-dozen ponds and hay feeding stations.

Only a handful of neighbors lived along that peaceful countryside, a hidden gem of a place in Mickey's memory. He remembered the girl who lived on that country road. His mind faded back fifty years or more to Nedra as a beautiful girl with sandy blonde hair and soft brown eyes. She was always outside in the tire swing hanging from the large oak just off from the porch. Her blue bicycle was faded by time and weather. There was a small thread of copper wire holding a handmade vanity tag just under the cracked seat. The rusty handlebars rested against her favorite shade tree. Nedra's sweet smile and enthusiasm caught Mickey's attention as a young boy. Each Saturday morning, Mickey would ride shotgun with his father, Emrick, to go pick up tobacco. Emrick enjoyed the tobacco and even generously offered it up to his crew and customers.

Mickey's father liked to arrive early to beat the large crowds, and Mickey didn't mind because he would get to watch Nedra cut the dried leaves like a pro. She would untie the large tobacco bales used to make Carolina cigarettes and Connecticut cigars. Nedra knew the difference in the leaves. She loved the heavy smell of the leaves and didn't mind the discoloration it would leave on her fingertips.

Mickey soon found himself beside her helping. Here, he managed to overcome his shyness. It was easy to talk when they were busy working, it didn't feel as awkward as it did when speaking face to face and making eye contact. Nedra talked enough for both of them. She was intelligent and a bit sassy, bubbling with confidence. Mickey was mesmerized by her demeanor. The girl was different and better than any lady he'd ever met.

Daniel and Emrick were entertained by the two of them dating. They witnessed Mickey as his arms looked like bananas after an hour of pushing Nedra in her tire swing. Harder and harder, he would push the tire as her dress flapped wildly in the wind. Their parents poured tea on the porch as the young man tried endlessly to impress Nedra with his strength. He would part his hair in the side mirror of Daniel's truck upon arrival. Nedra eventually aged out of the tire swing, took to picking flowers and walking the trails near the horses instead. Following her anywhere she went was Mickey, telling stories of being a great fisherman. He chuckled to himself about how hard she laughed when he stepped into a pile of manure. Together, they cleaned his shoes under an outside spigot near the well. She wasn't like any other girl in the world. Nedra was perfect. It was nearly ten miles from Whitemarsh Island to Randolph's home. Emrick made sure he had his son at Nedra's by nine o'clock as the men stood around, telling jokes and smoking cigars.

Rows of grass lined the abandoned train tracks where they trailed through the woods behind the barn. Wildflowers blanketed the landscape as far as the eye could see. Her mother, Annie, especially loved them. The two would spread the seeds over the fields like they were feeding her prize Rhode Island Reds. They giggled as the couple would jokingly say, "Here, chicky, chicky, chicky." Mickey liked that he could be silly with Nedra without embarrassment. She made him feel comfortable in his heart. Warm. Tender. Unbiased. Loved.

When Mickey was seventeen, his father took him down Tobacco Road for the long out of the way ride from Whitemarsh Island. He had no idea why his father loved tobacco so much. Emrick shared important talks with him about being a good fisherman and taking over the family business. He had no interest in hearing such nonsense at that age. His mind was somewhere else, waiting to hear Nedra's voice and to hold her hand. He begged his dad to press the pedal and hurry along. "Gas it to the end of the road," Mickey requested. He leaned forward on the dashboard. "Faster, dad."

"Be there shortly," replied Emrick. "Hold your horses." His father knew what was crossing his son's mind. Saturday mornings were the only time Mickey visited her because of school and fishing. One Saturday morning, as the Starr's were buying their tobacco, Daniel waved Mickey over and handed him the keys to his new truck.

"It's your turn, Mickey." Her father opened his hand. Nedra elbowed her boyfriend. "Go on," said Daniel. "Take Nedra for a ride."

"Are you sure, sir?" said Mickey, cranking the truck with Nedra beside him.

Daniel, Annie, and Emrick watched him drive down Tobacco Road. Halfway down the road was when Nedra scooted close to him as they drove together for the first time. She carried most of the conversation as he concentrated on the dusty road. As the couple slowed to make a U-turn and journey back home, she leaned over and kissed him. Mickey parked the truck. He liked how she made him feel, well, comfortable, so he kissed her back.

In June of '48, Mickey graduated from high school. Destined to serve his country as his forefathers had done, but against his parent's wishes, he joined the Army. His mother, Leona, cried for a week. Fourteen months after he shipped out, the wounded soldier packed his bags. Nedra was excited that he was coming home early but was disturbed that his premature arrival was due to a war-torn leg injury. He arrived in Savannah limping on a cane after taking a bullet in the thigh just after crossing the infamous "Bridge of No Return," known as the 38th parallel north. Mickey tried to make light of his experience in the hot zone of hell in North Korea by renaming it the "Bridge of One Return," laughing each time he told it at the tobacco barn. The wound discharged the soldier from further military action, where he was awarded the Purple Heart. Now a veteran of foreign war, he felt unsettled to leave behind his band of brothers to fight in Korea.

Daniel greeted Mickey at the door. "Welcome home, soldier," he said, shaking his hand. "It's good to see you, Starr."

Still dressed in his ASU, Mickey impulsively blurted out, "I'd take care of your daughter and work hard for her, sir." His bravery left, and his anxiety stepped in. He stuttered with words he'd practiced while overseas.

Daniel sensed where the conversation was headed and decided to rib Mickey by playing coy. "What are you saying, son?" He gestured, "Maybe you should sit down for a minute."

"Do you mind if I stand, sir? Mickey was nervous and shaken, mustering up strength, he took a deep breath. "I guess what I'm trying to say, Mr. Randolph, is that I'd like your blessing to marry Nedra."

"Does she know about this?" Daniel teased the young man. He knew the conversation with Mickey would happen sooner or later. "Are you sure you're ready? Marriage is a big step, and you just got home from the war, son."

"It is, Sir. I think I'm ready," the soldier stammered. "I mean, I know I'm ready."

Daniel chuckled, "No man is ready for marriage, but you have my permission, Mickey. Make sure you talk this over with Nedra."

Mickey didn't register Daniel's reply and mindlessly asked, "Do you need time to think about it, sir?"

"No, I already said yes, boy. Honestly, what does she see in you?" Daniel stood and extended his hand. "Welcome to the family, Mickey Starr."

Mickey shook his hand hard and repeated the words, 'thank you,' over and over. Daniel smirked.

"I'll take good care of her," he nodded. "You can count on it."

"I know you will, son," Daniel walked back to the barn. "You better." Daniel rested his arm atop Mickey's shoulders, pointing him toward Nedra, seated on the front porch. Nedra eagerly took the name Starr, three months later.

8

Just For You, 1995

Mickey was up early drinking coffee and reading the paper. Images of the Tobacco Barn flashed through his mind. His heart was breaking without Nedra as their anniversary was just a few short days away. Nedra and Mickey held such fond memories of the barn and the old oak tree where the two took Mickey's pocket knife and carved their names. After Annie and Daniel passed, Mickey and Nedra both poured their heart and soul into the Starr family fishing industry.

In a somewhat regretful decision, Nedra chose to part with her old homestead to loosen some cash flow for the expanding fishing business. This deal allowed Mickey to triple his boat fleet, but it also meant she had to part with her family home. Nedra found solace in that the new owner granted them unlimited access to the property. The buyer viewed the business deal as temporary assuming Mickey would soon repurchase the house. In loving-kindness, the new owner saved the place and respectfully left it intact. Nedra and Mickey never shared the deed exchange with their family as they planned to gain the property back one day, but as the business grew, the family spent less time on the farm and more time on the water. Time ticked on, and the plan to repurchase the homestead slipped further behind.

Mickey's drive to become the most esteemed seafood baron was halted. Inside, Nedra felt the memories of the barn and land were worth more than seafood, but the upkeep of both was impossible. Nedra hid her reluctance to let the place go, but truth be told, she would also never pass up an opportunity to support her husband's dream to building a fishing empire. Mickey thrived after the property sold, a lavish lifestyle was in their future. He was generous to Nedra, and they became closer. Although she preferred a more modest and straightforward approach to life, she adored how Mickey relished in doting on her. She fully accepted that extravagance was the fuel that burned his passion and zeal for their fishing business. Thankfully, the indifference to money didn't divide the happy couple and was never seen as a source of contention.

For their anniversary, Mickey generally contemplated purchasing Nedra a new piece of jewelry. He enjoyed giving her shiny trinkets and silver bracelets though she rarely wore them. Nedra told him that they were simply too fancy to wear around the house, and she would jokingly say that she was going to save them for when she gets all dolled up to go fishing. The two laughed about it.

Struggling with how to celebrate this year's anniversary without his beloved, he thought about the idea for days. He wanted to give Nedra something that she, herself, would genuinely cherish. Mickey sprang from the kitchen table, grabbed his camera, and headed outside. A picture of the lovebirds' favorite tree and some freshly picked wildflowers from behind The Tobacco Barn would be taken to her grave, where the two will celebrate.

Twenty years had passed, maybe more, but he remembered every little detail of the place. He planned for a beautiful vase to hold the flowers. Nedra would be thrilled; he felt her approval. Tears welled in his eyes as he envisioned her smiling down from heaven, and it gave him comfort.

He slid behind the wheel of his yellow '68 convertible Caddy, the car Nedra loved to take to Charleston. She requested he dropped the top as she tuned the radio to a station, and the two enjoyed South Carolina. Daniel and Annie would be proud of their son-in-law for celebrating Nedra with flowers from their farm. Mickey parked the car on Tobacco Road and soaked up the grand view. Upon advancing the film, he lifted and practiced focusing the camera. He paused, realizing that Nedra's sweet fingers were the last to snap the shutter. Brushing his fingers across the camera button, the photographer reached into his shirt pocket to extract some bifocals. He first took some practice shots of the green and white sign that read, TOBACCO ROAD. It hadn't changed much except now it leaned more, likely due to the storms over the years. The aged sign needed an adjustment, grunting and moaning as he forced the post to a vertical position. "This is for you, Nedra," he said, tamping with dirt and rocks. He released a kiss-off to the white clouds from his fingertips. Nedra was a believer, and he trusted she was with the Lord, where she promised she'd wait on him.

The daylight splashed across the fields, leaving only a few areas where the sun hadn't yet shone. The country road felt lonesome without her head resting on his shoulder. "Life's not the same without you, babe." He lifted his eyes to the blue skyline as the sun lit up the eastern side of the gray-barked trees. Continuing the conversation with Nedra, he pretended she was by his side. "That used to be the old Finch farm," he said, looking to his left.

It was the first farm yet to be butchered or made into a subdivision. The old Anderson place posted four new homes on their property. He noticed, however, scanning the Colbert's farm, they hadn't given into expansion and commercialization. That 'old coot' was probably asking a fortune. Mickey feared the rest of the drive would be different than he had remembered. Three of the seven ponds were now dry, and one was filled in, level with the rest of the land with what looked to be fresh dirt. A yellow end loader was parked at Patterson's farm. "Well, that's not good," he expressed to Nedra. Only two more miles until he reached her homeplace.

Unforgiving storms had damaged three of the hanging oaks over the years. A terrible loss. One giant oak limb was drooping close to the ground, so the owner propped it up with pallets to prevent it from splitting. The lifespan of the large divine oaks was several hundred years. Mickey remembered his father's speech about the larger oaks of the South when he was a teenager. The small stream signaled to him that the drive was only a mile more.

Looking around, Mickey felt guilty about Nedra selling the real estate to expand his fishing operation. Now, he wished they would have kept it. The neighborhood had changed drastically, and he worried about the condition of the barn and land. He pulled slowly to a bare area near the house. Removing his glasses, staring out to soak it all in as the sun hit the front side of the giant barn doors, he saw the structure was now a sad relic. The place appeared gloomy and vacant. Leaves filled the porch where he used to swing with Nedra. She would think that it needed a broom and a fresh coat of paint. He opened a door and examined the inside of the barn. The wooden counters were still there, yet dusty. Hooks holding tobacco stalks remained in the same position now dirty and desolate.

Mickey was reminded of his childhood, and he imagined his father, proud and happy as he paid for his plug. He reminisced about the wedding and the tender conversation they had.

"Love ya, Mick," his father said.

"Love you too, Pops."

"I'm a little surprised you picked me as your best man, though."

"There was no better choice."

"I'm pleased that you did."

"Me too."

"We've had some good times; it tickles your mother when she thinks of us as best buddies." Emrick chuckled while hugging him.

"Pops, I never considered anyone else but you."

"Thank you, son, that means a lot to me. You're the best, you know that, Mick? Always thinking of others," said his father. "You sure picked a beautiful bride and a good lady."

"Don't I know it!"

Emerick glanced at his watch. "Just a few minutes before you say your vows."

"Not long now."

"She's a keeper, for sure," smiled Mickey.

He stood beside his son. "The first time I spoke to her, I liked her."

"She means the world to me. Thanks for helping me catch her."

The two laughed as they realized that they were using fishing jargon to describe his bride to be.

"Yep, she's special, Mick. Her parents are good people. Your mother likes her, too."

"Means a lot," sniffed Mickey with watery eyes.

Knock! Knock! Knock!

"Come in," called Mickey.

"Five minutes, groom," the wedding coordinator announced as she hugged him. "She's beautiful, just stunning. She said to tell you that she loves you more than anything in the world."

The coordinator's signal made Mickey a little nervous. As he stood before the guests, his mother's sweet smile and a nod of approval relaxed him.

Mickey turned to his father and said, "Thanks for not making me work on Saturdays."

He felt his father's hand on his back. "I knew she'd be good for you. Plus, who could pass up a chance to get the family discount on tobacco." He covered his mouth and laughed.

Mickey now stood outside where he'd once helped unload tobacco bales. Wiping his eyes with his fingers, he mouthed out loud, "Nedra, life is much harder down here without you." Familiar sites brought back a flood of memories, and he felt right about being there again. The man unsnapped his leather camera case and wrapped the handmade Aztec print shoulder strap around his neck. The sun found his face and warmed him. He felt incompetent in handling the complicated camera. Nedra usually mastered the photography and scrapbooked the pictures in a large binder.

The cool morning fog lifted above the wildflower fields as the horses ran in the distance. The land reminded him of the luxurious horse farms and stables he and Nedra photographed in Lexington, Kentucky, right before the big race. He pressed the button. Snap, cha-cha! Snap, cha-cha! Snap, cha-cha! The Savannah sky glowed with a warm orange tint, and light blue streaks stretched from over the hayfield to just above the Peterson's meadow.

It probably wouldn't be long before developers offered the owner a deal resulting in timbering the land and demolishing the house. The home was still in reasonably good shape considering its time on earth, and it saddened him to think of it becoming a subdivision. Mickey peeked through the windows to see the golden hardwood floors her dad cut and installed a year before he left for Korea. They were dulled by time, and the foot traffic had scuffed the clear coat down to the bare wood in places. The kitchen cabinets that Mickey made for Annie's fiftieth birthday still hung on the walls. The wood could use some sandpaper, and the hardware needed a good polishing, but they were still intact.

The man exited the porch and made his way toward the oak. "Now to our tree, Nedra." Twigs cracked from the weight of his hiking boots. Twice he stopped to rest. Tipp's nagging sounded in his head as his habit of smoking cigars and pipes prevented him from keeping a steady pace. Moving forward, he found the spring where Nedra would collect water for her daddy's coffee. Kneeling to drink the cold water from his hand, he remembered her cute smile. The crisp water refreshed him, and his desire was to spend the day beside the spring.

Plowing through a thick bed of fallen pine needles led him down a slight embankment opening into a field, he supported himself with small saplings, which kept him stable in the dense forest. He stood under the massive timber, comfortable and at peace, but still he missed her. The fields and woodlands brought her back to him, and he was happy he'd decided to make the long-overdue trek to the land where they once frolicked. She'd told him how she loved the flowers and trees in the field more than city streets and shopping downtown. It was then that he understood how nature sang to Nedra's soul.

He stopped to tend to a cut he sustained from an overgrown briar patch. Through the brush, he thought he saw Nedra leaning against a Poplar tree eating blackberries. He rounded the tree; her figure was gone. "Nedra!" he paused, scoping the forest. Shouting again, "Nedra! come back to me." Mickey squinted his eyes and scanned one last time. Disappointed, he ventured on. Their favorite tree had to be around here somewhere, Mickey thought. He hoped it was still alive and standing taller and broader.

A few steps further and there it stood, recognizing it immediately. "There's our Love Oak, Nedra," he sighed with relief. He couldn't help but think if Nedra was guiding him right to it. Mickey hurried over to examine the carvings. The warmth of the sunshine had dried and cracked the bark. Red-headed woodpeckers had drilled holes above their names, but the letters were undisturbed. He pressed his cheek against the rough bark and closed his eyes. Mickey was unclear of his emotions, he felt it was a tortured and broken happiness. He found solace in feeling her presence, but it made him long for her even more. The loneliness consumed him. Tears dripped from the corners of his eyes. "Happy Anniversary, babe. I miss you," Mickey spoke softly.

He opened his eyes and gently traced his fingers across the words, "Mickey loves Nedra." Overwhelmed with grief, he struck the tree several times with his fist. Blood dripped from his knuckles. He snapped a picture of the tree and picked enough flowers for Nedra and Shasta. Hundreds. He adjusted his thin jacket around his shoulders, and one last time, traced each letter in her name and outlined the heart before stepping back to snap more pictures. Upon twisting the lens to narrow its focus, placing his finger atop the shutter button, he then adjusted his stance. Mickey pressed the button. Nothing. Trying again, nothing. He examined the camera and realized it was jammed. Not much could be done in the middle of the woods, without tools. Besides, he'd be too afraid to open it for fear of exposing the film. He was desperate. At that moment, he'd given it all up to finish his life with her. Mickey decided to lean on Nedra's God. Speaking aloud in an unfamiliar way, he yelled, "Umm God, uh Lord upstairs, I wish somehow or someway, if you wouldn't mind, uh that I could just step back in time and hold her again. Please, sir, please. Just for a minute. It's too hard to live without her." He hoped that if the Lord didn't grant his request, at least He would relay the message to her. The wait for a response was horrendous, but deep down, he knew his wish wouldn't be granted. Saddened, the old man hung his head and began the hike back up the hill to the barn.

A humming in the background sounded like a running chainsaw. The noise began to trail in closer. Mickey saw an ATV headed down the hill in his direction.

"Must be someone setting up a tree stand," he thought. As the rider approached, a big man canted his head with a sharp smirk. "Is that you, Mickey Starr?"

"Yep, it's me."

"I thought that was your junky '68 Caddy parked at the top of the hill."

"Carter Cigar," he scoffed. "What are you doing here?" Mickey scanned the area for a good-sized stick or a rock for protection.

"You're trespassing on my land!" Carter shook his head while pooching out his lips that held an unlit stub of a cigar.

"How did you get it? Did something happen to..."

Carter interrupted Mickey and told him his intention. "I'm putting the Tobacco Barn in my name, already started the paperwork."

The old man was devastated to hear the news, and his chest began to tighten. Mickey resisted the urge to grab his chest in front of his enemy despite the pain.

"Oh, that's right, this used to be your daddy-in-law's property," he scowled, popping his knuckles. "Daniel Randolph, right? He sold diseased tobacco, ripped people off for years," he said accusingly, spitting on the ground. "Glad he died!"

"You watch your damn mouth, Carter! You know that's not true." Mickey slowly lowered his camera to the ground and grabbed a rock in the process. His nostrils expanded as he planned his first move to fight the big man.

"Where's Tipp? Where's your crew?" asked Carter, perched on the ATV. "There's nobody here to back your sorry ass up." He hopped off the machine. "And I'm not going to feel bad when I beat your ass down." Carter walked toward Mickey and clenched his fist. Carter Cigar was a long-haired, sloppy-looking redneck. A boat thief who could barely read and write his own name. Mickey summoned his military training and remained calm as he assumed his position.

"I've got you now, and nobody's around to witness it!" Carter grunted and swung at Mickey's skull. Mickey fired back and landed a hard hit to the side of Carter's head with a rock. Three quick jabs to Carter's mid-section caught him off guard, eliminating his ability to return a punch. Carter plunged to the ground.

"Get up, Carter!" shouted Mickey. "You do a lot of talking, it's time to put an end to your stealing off people." Sweat dripped from Mickey's face. "And bad-mouthing dead people, you're disgusting!" Mickey landed a kick as Carter plundered around, attempting to get up.

Carter sat on the ground, scowling at Mickey as he wiped the blood from his head. Carter grabbed Mickey's pant leg causing him to lose his balance. He hit the ground, shoving the camera under a pile of leaves before scrambling to his feet.

"Damn you, Carter!"

Mickey's forearm dripped blood from a fresh cut obtained from falling.

"It feels good to watch the great Mickey Starr suffer."

Now standing, Carter swung a stick that landed against his neck, leaving a gaping wound. He kicked the side of Carter's knee, knocking it out of place just as Carter landed a hard hit. Mickey fell backward, slamming into the ground. His hand patted the ground feeling for his camera. Carter climbed aboard the ATV and drove off slinging dirt and leaves on top of Mickey. "You're not worth my energy," shouted Carter from behind the handlebars. On the ground, his ears were ringing, and his vision tunneled. Mickey blacked out and lost consciousness. Carter returned in less than ten minutes, rolling Mickey's limp body onto the ATV cargo rack. The fractured man was then dumped into the back seat of his yellow convertible. Carter glanced over his shoulder to see if anyone had witnessed the event. To make a final strike, Carter lifted the man's wallet and quickly fled the scene.

***

When Tipp woke after sunrise, he went to the kitchen to start a pot of coffee as Volt and Terry, Volt's younger brother slept in. The men stayed up late the night before visiting as Terry had arrived in town. Stepping into the kitchen, Tipp saw a note on the kitchen bar.

Tipp,

I'm headed to the Tobacco Barn to take a few pictures. You boys get your set ready and start practicing for the concert. Raquel has the day off, so don't mess up her kitchen. She left fresh orange juice in the fridge and bagels in the bread keeper for you. I'll see you around lunchtime.

~M

Tipp knew Mickey was having heart trouble lately, and he didn't like the idea of him being away and alone. The barn was a remote area with help and medical care amiss. He wished Mickey would've asked him to go. Tipp paced the kitchen, wondering whether to stay with the guys or go check on his grandpa. There was an unsettling feeling he couldn't shake. With the note in hand, Tipp raced to wake the guys.

"Hey, Volt!" shouted Tipp. "Y'all get up!"

"What's wrong?"

"Well, nothing I hope, but grandpa's gone off on his own, and I just don't like him being alone with his bad heart." Tipp handed the note to Volt. "Ride with me so you can drive his car back home. He's got no business driving right now. Wake up Terry, and let's take off."

"Sure, man. I'll get Terry up," replied Volt. Terry was half-asleep when Volt knocked on the door. "I'm up," he said after Volt explained what was going on. He stepped into the hallway a few minutes later dressed and ready to go.

"All right, let's go," Terry said, handing the keys to his Suburban to Tipp.

"Tipp, what's this about a big concert?" Volt asked, looking at his friend.

Tipp sighed. "It's a long story. I'll tell you on the way.

"Okay, but let me run over and see if Shasta wants to ride with us instead of going later," Volt added as he ran down the street to the McGregor's house.

9

Bruised and Burned

Wait, what's his name? The singer from North Carolina? Volt Hendricks, right?" Mr. McGregor touched his thin beard.

"What? Who?" Mrs. McGregor asked, "Volt, who?"

"Why Shasta Kay McGregor, what in the world?"

Shasta raised her voice and rolled her eyes. "Gee, thanks, Dad!" She punched his left arm.

"Yes, Mother, I'm dating Volt Hendricks, the singer. Nothing is secret around here. Thanks to my father!" She walked to her room, shouting, "I'm not twelve anymore!"

Her mother turned to her husband with her hands on her hips.

"When did this happen?" She smoothed a strand of hair back onto the top of her head. "Was I asleep? Rick, how did you know about our daughter, and I didn't?"

Mr. McGregor shrugged his shoulders, "I don't know anything," he replied, walking down the hall to the bedroom.

"They were kissing on the front steps last night. That's all I know. The last guy was a football player. Before him a rockstar or a geologist or a Russian spy? I can't keep up."

Shasta opened her bedroom door, "Volt is different, dad."

"Oh yeah, they're all different, but they're all the same too. Just ask Raquel, she'll tell you the truth about all guys."

"So, tell me, Rick, what is this truth about all guys?" Mrs. McGregor scowled at her husband, placing her hands back on her hips. Shasta stepped into the hallway and said, "No, he's different. I promise you that much. I met him at Mickey's party."

Her mother spoke while brushing her teeth, "Mickey had a big party, and we weren't invited?"

Shasta combed her hair and stepped behind the mirror. "That would be uncomfortable, Mother. My parents out with a guy that I'm being introduced to. I don't think so. Besides, it was a blind dinner date, not a big party."

Shasta closed her door and changed clothes. "It just happened."

"It better not have happened," her mother's voice got loud.

Mr. McGregor chuckled, kissing his wife, as she walked over to where her daughter was standing. Shasta shared secrets with her mother, but never to her father. She whispered into her mother's ear, "We hit it off and talked by the pool. This morning, we are going to pick flowers for the pageant at Tybee

Island." Her mother held up the clothes Shasta had lying on her bed. "Where are you going to pick flowers?"

"At Miss Nedra's barn."

Ding dong, the doorbell sounded. "I'll bet that is Mr. Volt Hendricks himself," said Mrs. McGregor eagerly. "I want to meet him."

"I'll get it!" Shasta yelled. "That's my date."

She rushed to answer the door.

"Good morning, Shasta, Mr. McGregor, Mrs. McGregor," Volt spoke briskly. "I hate to be rude and in a rush, but we think Mickey might need some help. I wanted to let you know that I may not be able to pick flowers with you. The boys and I are going to head over to the Tobacco Barn and check on Mickey. He should have been back home a while ago."

"What? Need some help?" asked Mr. McGregor.

"What can we do?" offered Mrs. McGregor. "Is it his heart again?"

Shasta slipped on her shoes.

"We need to go," responded Volt, checking his watch. "Clock is ticking."

Shasta waved to her parents inside the doorway. "Let's go, I'm ready."

"See you later, Mr. and Mrs. McGregor," Volt said with a raised hand. The doors slammed after Volt helped Shasta into Terry's vehicle.

"Where do you think he is, Tipp?" asked Shasta.

"Somewhere between here and Tobacco Road, I assume." Tipp spun the tires and yanked the shifter into gear. "Too many hoodlums use the area to store their black-market goods because it's so isolated. It's just not good to be there alone, won't be anybody around to help him if he needs it."

Terry adjusted his seatbelt and listened to the conversation.

"Shasta, this is my little brother, Terry," said Volt, introducing the two. "Terry, this is Shasta, she's Mickey's next-door neighbor and uh, well, my umm," he nervously stammered.

Shasta interrupted the awkward moment, "I'm Volt's girlfriend. Good to meet you, Terry," she answered abruptly while reaching her hand towards Terry from the back seat of the vehicle. The group laughed collectively then took turns teasing Volt.

"There's a barn," pointed Volt, trying to change the topic.

"No, that's not it, we're on Spencer Road, it's about two more miles down," replied Tipp.

Volt rolled down the window and enjoyed the view as they drove closer to the property.

"Oh good, there's Mickey's Cadillac," alerted Shasta.

The group came to a halt and scurried out all four doors of the vehicle. Shasta noticed something on the side of Mickey's car. "Oh my God!" she screamed. "Is that blood?"

"That's blood alright," said Terry, examining the red matter dripping from the door.

"He must have cut himself," deduced Shasta.

"I've seen enough cuts in jail, bar fights and with gang bangers to know, that's not a paper cut," admitted Terry.

"Mickey! Help!" screamed Shasta. "He's in the car. Oh my God, help him!" Shasta stood with her hands on the sides of her face, paralyzed in fear.

Volt and Tipp scrambled over the sides of the vehicle to get to Mickey. Terry grabbed a pistol from his glove box and scouted the property.

"Grandpa! Grandpa!" Tipp tapped Mickey's cheeks and shook his shoulders. "He's unconscious and in bad shape!" he yelled. "Blood is coming out of his ears, Tipp," warned Volt. Shasta trembled, feeling helpless.

"Oh, God, it's a pool of blood under his head. He's lost a lot of blood," said Volt. "We need to get help, now!"

"Poor, Mickey," said Shasta as tears fell from her eyes. "Let's get him inside the truck and take him to the hospital."

Tipp opened the door. Volt climbed in the back and helped lift Mickey across the back seat. Shasta cleaned the blood from Mickey's face with her blouse. The man's head flopped, and was still unresponsive. The group had no idea of how long he had been hurt. His face was swollen and hardly recognizable.

Terry returned from scouting the property. "There's no one here, he yelled. Both of his hands are bloody, the man was in one hell of a fight, but Mickey is a tough old goat."

They banked on him, pulling through if they could get him medical attention, quickly.

"Put him in the back seat," Shasta bellowed as she ran ahead to open the door.

Tipp placed the trunk of Mickey's body on the back seat as Volt and Terry pulled him across to the other side. Shasta slid under Mickey's head and held it on their way to the hospital. Volt held Mickey's legs while Tipp and Terry took the two front seats. Shasta sobbed, "He needs to go to the emergency room and fast. I'll take care of you, Mickey," Shasta whispered as she stroked his hair. "You're like a grandfather to me," she continued, looking at him for any sign of movement. "You mean the world to me." She pushed a strand of hair that had fallen in her face behind her ear with a blood-soaked hand. She briefly glanced out the truck window and had a private talk with God.

"This has Carter Cigar written all over it!" blurted Tipp, completely pissed at the thought.

Shasta's jeans and shirt were saturated with blood.

"Start the truck, Tipp, let's go," said Terry as Tipp clambered for the keys.

Tipp cranked the engine. "Nothing. It's not turning over." Tipp stared at Terry. "What's wrong with your truck, Terry?" Both men squinted, sporting long, sour faces.

"Someone's coming down the road." Shasta moved behind Tipp's shoulder to gain a better view of the approaching vehicle. "Look."

Panicking, Volt stressed, "We don't have much time, guys."

Terry motioned for the two to swap places, and he climbed behind the wheel. Terry banged the steering column with his hand, jerking and cranking the wheel. "Sometimes, it sticks. Come on, baby, start! It'll fire up, hang on," Terry assured his friends. "The engine turned over."

"Mickey moved his legs!" shouted Volt.

"Can you hear me, Mickey? Mickey? Wake up, Mickey," Shasta pleaded as she stroked his head. "Mickey, can you hear me?" she asked, tilting his head. "Get us to the hospital, *please*, Terry."

"Fast as I can." Terry spun out and darted to the end of Tobacco Road. "Which way, guys?" He yelled. "What's the fastest route to the hospital?"

"Take a left, here," directed Tipp.

Terry checked for traffic and blazed down Tobacco Road.

"Turn on your emergency flashers," warned Tipp. "Watch for cows and horses in the road."

"We can come back later and get his car," said Volt.

"Before dark, though," Shasta said. "If this has anything to do with Carter Cigar, he's bad news, I've heard." She cleaned the blood on Mickey's face.

"He's looking better," Tipp told her. "Thank you for looking after my grandpa. Ten more minutes to the hospital from here," Tipp told Terry.

***

When the ER staff lifted Mickey onto a gurney, his battered body was still unresponsive. The group was not sure how much time had passed since Mickey sustained his injuries. Each of them played out a different scenario of what possibly happened.

So many questions were unanswered. Talking to the medical staff was a blur for Tipp; he was shaken. Due to the nature of the injuries, police were called to investigate. The group helped give information, in hopes of finding the person who attacked Mickey.

Volt neglected to remember that Shasta was assisting with a pageant that night in Tybee Island. Never mentioning the pageant, Shasta eagerly agreed to stay with Mickey at the hospital. The three men jumped into the bloodstained vehicle and headed back to the Tobacco Barn.

As Tipp pulled up next to Mickey's car, they noticed something odd about the condition of the Caddy prompting Volt and Terry to jump out. The men stood tall and scanned the fields, ensuring they were alone as Terry grabbed a flashlight from a toolbox in the back of his vehicle and handed it to Tipp.

"Guys, this son of a bitch has burned the car to the damn ground," said Tipp. "It's as black as West Virginia coal."

"What kind of senseless bastard does this to a Cadillac?" Tipp shouted at the top of his lungs.

"One that needs his ass kicked," yelled Terry, examining the slightly opened trunk barely lit by the vehicle headlights. "I wish the sons of bitches would show up for just five minutes!" He waved his gun.

"We just missed those bastards, too!" yelled Volt.

"Look at the truck tracks and the dipping oil, it's fresh evidence." Tipp pointed down at a dark mud hole. The drizzle revealed clues on the soil, exposing extra-wide tire marks. Walking around the barn, Tipp scanned the field, waving a flashlight and hoped to find someone.

"Let's go, I wanna get back," said Tipp. "Besides, I know who it was. Only one person round here that cold-blooded and cruel enough to pull a stunt like this anyways."

Smoke from the unsettling fresh burn rolled from the seats and trunk of Mickey's car. The guys climbed back in the vehicle, disappointed and full of rage. They made their way back to the hospital, hoping to hear good news from Shasta and the doctor. The men returned to find Mickey hooked up to an IV and a heart monitor. His cuts had been addressed, and Tipp was incredibly relieved to hear from the nurse that his heart rhythm was beating steadily.

It was a long evening at the hospital. "I want to stay with Mickey tonight," offered Shasta. "I can come back as soon as the pageant is over." She took the last bite of her chicken dinner from the cafeteria. "Mr. and Mrs. Starr practically raised me, anyways. Besides, my mom is already on her way to sit with him so that I can go home to shower and change."

"No, no," Tipp insisted. "I'll stay with Mickey."

"I'd like to, if possible?" she repeated her intention, then took a drink of her soda. "You can go home and rest when I return."

"Alright." Tipp nodded and appreciated her care. "He'll be better soon," Tipp said with hope, but deep inside, he was worried sick about the old man.

10

Harvest Moon

Towering coastal lighthouses and beautiful landscapes drew large crowds to the heart of the South. Visitors poured into coastal areas of Georgia on the weekends. Seaport communities were hot spots to meet with friends for drinks on weekends, and couples enjoyed music and romantic sunsets. For the Lowcountry, saltwater and seafood were undeniable blessings of coastal living. Feeling better, Mickey was released from the hospital on the conditions of following a strict concussion protocol.

Blue skies stretched over Tybee Island, and the day was a perfect one to be outside.

"I have a big surprise for you," said Shasta, running in Volt's direction and jumping into his arms.

He held her hands to his side. "What is it? As excited as you are, this has to be good," he said, bending to kiss her.

"I've waited all day to tell you," she whispered. "I want to take you to the ocean."

Volt's voice elevated. "The ocean? Not a steak dinner or some cheesy romantic movie? I've spent the last ten hours on the water working with Tipp and Terry. I'm supposed to be on leave," he chuckled.

"This is with me, though," she moaned in his ear. "You and I will be under the moonlight together." She moved closer. A seductive look overtook her face. While pulling on his shirt, a button popped loose and rolled across the driveway. Her energy surprised him, and he gave Shasta a curious look.

Volt smiled, asking, "What was that about?"

Terry walked up behind his brother with an empty lunch box in one hand and the button in the other. "It's going to be a good night for you, soldier."

"Just watch and learn," boasted Volt.

"I didn't mean to do that to your shirt. I was just playing with you, like in the movies."

Volt pulled her close and kissed her neckline, enjoying the way she flirted with him.

"Let's keep going since you already started to unbuttoned my shirt." Volt opened the rest of his shirt as a joke.

"Not here," she said, stepping back to wave at Tipp as he slammed the tailgate on his truck and walked inside the mudroom. "But soon," said Shasta, holding his hand. "I promise."

"I can wait," he said, kissing her forehead as she moved her hands under his shirt. Volt liked how her hands gently stroked his back, adoring the look in her puppy dog eyes.

"But I thought it would be nice for us to take a stroll on the beach. Just relax and have fun." The evening breeze started to cool down on the coast. "We haven't walked on the beach together yet."

"Let's kickback on a blanket with a few beverages," he suggested. "Watch the sunset and the waves crash."

Shasta rubbed his chest with her pink painted nails, and his abs flexed against her fingertips when her hands descended. She stepped back and took a deep breath, then tugged at her long wavy hair.

"Whew, I'm tired," moaned Volt. "Terry and I are helping Tipp and Mickey with fishing and man, it's harder than basic training."

Her face appeared disappointed. "If you don't want to go," she said with sad eyes, "we can do something else."

Volt watched how quickly her demeanor changed. "Tipp said there's a nice bistro next to the pier and the chef is from Charleston, they make the best crab dip in town. Maybe we can try it," he said, not wanting to disappoint her.

Shasta perked up at his suggestion. "Okay, and I know you like crab dip, and we both love music."

"You are starting to pay attention to the food I like," said Volt. "That's impressive."

Her hand slipped down into his belt loop. "On Saturdays, they have music, and open mic night, maybe you could sing for little ole' me?" Shasta stood on her tiptoes, kissing him.

"I believe I'm up for it," he said and grinned at the thought.

"Oh my God, the great Volt Hendricks is going to sing at Tybee Island!"

"If they will let me."

"Oh, they will let you." She gripped his hand and squeezed. "I'm sure of that. You have a record deal!"

He brushed his hand through her hair. "I'll take my guitar just in case they ask me."

They walked down the driveway to Mickey's front door. She looked up at him, touching the tip of his nose with her finger.

"I can't believe you are going to sing tonight! The audience will freak out when they see you on stage."

Shasta jumped, and Volt lifted her through the doorway on his back. "I'd love to sing for you. Perhaps somewhere private," hinting seductively.

"Well, Mr. Hendricks, you're so bold and forward. Soon, very soon, but first, you should grab a shower. A cold one." Shasta teased, gently pushing him away.

***

An hour later, Volt grabbed his guitar, picked up Shasta, and the two headed out. She leaned on him in the truck and closed her eyes as he drove from Whitemarsh to Tybee Island.

"This island is a beautiful place, isn't it?"

"Yeah, I like it. Great seafood, right?"

Shasta responded quickly, "The best!"

Across the mainland, east of Savannah was the twenty-mile stretch of Tybee Island. Lining the streets on both sides of Highway 80 were surf shops, trendy boutiques, and a place to sample the coldest beer in the world. Kids would flock to the ice cream shop at the corner market near the Tybee Pier, and the adults enjoyed live entertainment on the weekends.

The couple dined on Savannah's signature shrimp and grits. Shasta enjoyed a glass of white wine with her meal while he drank his weight in southern sweet tea. After dinner, Volt grabbed his guitar from the truck, surprised the audience as he took the stage and sang two songs. He was pleased with the feedback he received from the unassuming audience. It felt good to play to a new and different crowd. The standing roar made him feel invincible. Volt waved, walking off the small wooden stage, and taking Shasta's soft hand to head to the dunes. Volt placed his guitar in his truck as Shasta ran inside a souvenir shop to purchase a blanket for the beach. The two met back at the boardwalk and traversed across the cool sand until finding a place to relax.

"I bet you can't find seafood like that in Highlands or Troutman," she said, hooking her arm around his to maintain balance.

He pulled her close and moved his arm to grip the shoulders of her small frame. "Well," Volt chuckled, "I thought you would brag about my singing first, but I see that I can't compare with coastal shrimp and grits."

Laughing and embarrassed, Shasta was defensive, "Oh no, I didn't mean..."

Volt abruptly interrupted. "I'm just kidding, you're right. The food and the company were fantastic, but the singing was mediocre." The two snickered. "I guess I had to come here to find the good stuff, didn't I?"

"Awwww, you are sweet," she said, placing her head on his chest and closing her eyes, "you know that?"

Her hands felt soft and tender on his rough skin.

"I'm glad you're finished singing in the bistro, though."

"Why?" he asked, turning in her direction. "Was it *that* bad? Are you not a fan?" He examined her eyes while waiting for a response.

"The blonde at the bar was undressing you with her eyes."

Shaking his head side to side, he asked, "What's the big deal about her?"

Placing her hand on her hip, Shasta uttered, "I overheard the blonde tell the brunette how she wanted to take you home for a private concert."

"Oh, Lord, that's crazy." He laughed, rubbing his mustache. "Besides, I don't take requests."

A tight grin slowly crept onto her face. Suppressing the smile, Shasta responded, "It's not funny, Volt."

While running, Volt replied, "You're right, it's downright hilarious! Remember, I'm at home in your arms." He touched her face with his lips when she caught up. "I'm just fine right here."

Within a few minutes, a tangerine sun dropped out of sight, and the rising tide eased up to their toes as they splashed each other.

"Let's put down the blanket in front of the boardwalk." She picked a nice spot near the dunes. "You can see that last bit of sunlight setting the town aglow from here. It's nice, right?"

"There's nothing better than a sunset at Tybee Island."

Volt opened the blanket and spread it on the sand with Shasta holding her corners. The two crashed onto the blanket.

"Listen to the ocean," he said, It's soothing. Makes me feel so relaxed. A person could get used to this kind of life."

He smiled and winked at Shasta, stroking his hand across her forehead to sweep the breeze blown bangs from her face. He continued to massage her shoulders and tanned neckline.

"That's my sweet spot." She closed her eyes as her head fell into his body.

"Good," added Volt, smiling. He massaged her back while gently kissing her shoulders. Her neckline had a sweet fruity fragrance. He remembered it from the night they met. He liked it. Whispering he said, "You smell great, I love that scent."

"I was hoping you would."

The deck lights came on at the beach house nearby, and Volt turned his head to relax onto his stomach, part of the blanket covered his face. Suddenly, a group of sorority girls rushed down the boardwalk. Flashlights waved back and forth like the police had evacuated their house from a blazing fire. The girls screamed as they ran past the couple, kicking up sand and broken seashells as they ran down the soft beach sand.

"Watch kicking the sand, please!" Shasta yelled, visibly annoyed by the girls, who cramped their romantic evening.

"Excuse me." The girl in the front slowed down. "I'm so sorry, ma'am." The polite young girl stepped back and proceeded to brush the sand from the corner of their beach blanket with her hand.

Shasta flagged down one of the girls at the end of the pack. "Is the place on fire?" she asked. "What's going on?"

"Volt Hendricks is playing at the bistro." She started running to catch up with her girlfriends. "We're all headed down to see him and get his autograph. You should come with us!" she shouted as she ran toward the glowing lights of the bustling bistro.

"Thank you, but I'm not a big fan of Volt Hendricks," Shasta hid her smile with her hands. In a curious turn, Volt rolled over into her hands and laughed.

"What do you mean you're not a big fan?"

Shasta sarcastically asked, "Speaking of your biggest fan, how's Brandi doing?"

"How do you know, Brandi?"

"She's my cousin, and trust me, I'm not proud of being her relative." Shasta snarled her lips and scoffed.

"Brandi went back to college in Greenville, South Carolina," said Volt with a low voice. "We didn't stay in touch with each other. Our relationship faded away, and we broke up." Volt rubbed the back of his neck, saying, "That was pretty much it, I guess."

He placed his hand under Shasta's chin to initiate a kiss, but after talking about Brandi, Shasta turned cold and tightened her lips. Feeling discontent, she removed her hand from his side. Volt hadn't known her for very long, but he knew when a woman was mad as hell.

"Why are we talking about me?" He traced the lines in his palm. "Didn't you date a pro football player?" he asked. "Maybe we should stop while we're ahead."

"Good idea," agreed Shasta.

They both realized that discussing past relationships made them jealous, and they respected each other's past.

Changing the subject, Shasta asked, "Want some ice cream from the shop we saw earlier or a cold beer? I'm craving a banana split."

"Sounds good. Let's go."

Sand fell from the blanket as they shook it loose and pocketed three nice shells. They headed for the boardwalk. The cool water from the spigot felt refreshing as the couple rinsed the sand from their feet and legs. Volt picked Shasta up and hoisted her onto the railing so she could put on her sandals. She placed her hand inside his when he helped her down. Enamored by Volt's chivalrous acts, Shasta smiled meekly at him.

"You're devastatingly handsome, you know that?"

"I have to impress you somehow."

The short ride gave them another opportunity to discover each other. It was a little deeper, more heartfelt conversation than before. In two weeks, they'd talked about their favorite foods and places they'd visited, but there was still more to uncover. Shasta was interesting and Volt liked the way she cared for Mickey. She appreciated his kindness and how he picked wildflowers and helped others when they were in trouble.

After he parked in downtown, Shasta spotted a horse and buggy ride rolling through the cobblestone streets of historic Savannah. Couples seemed to be in love with the city.

"I love horses, don't you?"

"I do like certain breeds," he said, holding her hand. "My father has a black stallion on our farm in Highlands."

"A white buggy being pulled by a black horse is so romantic," she said, squeezing his hand. Volt spotted a couple in a horse and buggy, the groom was dressed in a black and white tux, and the bride seemed to be enjoying the ride in her long white wedding veil, blowing in the breeze."

"Cuddled up like they'd been together forever," said Volt.

"Happy." He stared until they were out of sight. "They are content, aren't they?"

She sighed, watching the driver flip and roll the reins, on his way to the river walk.

"Isn't Savannah the most enchanting town in the world?"

"Stunning, like you," he charmed her, as the traffic light changed from red to green.

"I get a little jealous when I see happy couples together."

Shasta watched a cute older man help his wife load shopping bags in a nearby buggy and roll away.

"Why?"

"I want the same romance for myself," she said, "I want to fall in love again."

Volt turned to her, holding her hand. "We could fall in love, you know?"

"I know we could."

When they walked passed the pizza pub Volt had an idea. "I'll be back in a minute," he said.

Shasta located a bench and sat. "I'll wait here for you."

Volt walked around the corner, out of Shasta's sight. He stood for ten minutes before he reached the front of the line.

"Yes sir, I'd like to book a buggy for two." He smiled. "It doesn't have to be a tour or anything fancy, just a stroll in the park, if possible?"

The booking agent checked the schedule and replied, "Why young man, I have a buggy that will be back in about ten minutes or so. We can fit you on a romantic ride for two."

The stocky gray-haired man tipped his black hat. "That's a good deed, for a nice lady, I bet?" He acknowledged back with a handshake to Volt.

"You've seen this done before?"

"A hundred times a day," said the man.

"Does it work?" questioned Volt.

"Every time," the gentleman added, "I'll get you a ride through the historic district, including Chippewa Square."

"Good," said Volt. "I appreciate the Southern hospitality."

"Sir, you look so familiar," the man said, tugging at his ear. "I've seen you before," he claimed, looking through his specs, "Not sure where, though?"

"This should cover it," Volt said, handing him the money.

"See you in ten minutes. Thanks for the tip, Sonny."

Shasta was sitting under a sugar maple when the drizzle started to fall on her head. Volt noticed her hair getting wet, so he offered to buy an umbrella, but she declined and moved further under the tree to block the raindrops. He grabbed her hand and led her to the buggy.

The driver extended his hand toward Shasta. "Don't you two make a dashing couple? Little lady, you are a stunning beauty."

"You are gracious with words," remarked Shasta. "Nice to meet you, sir."

Volt relaxed into the corner of the buggy.

Before the driver pulled the reins on the horse, he turned to speak to his guests. "The clouds are moving in, but it looks like it will be a peaceful ride for two lovebirds. The missus has me keep a soft blue afghan in the seat, if you'd like to use it, you're welcome to it."

"Appreciate it," said Shasta, shivering. "The wind has picked up; I think I'll take you up on that offer."

The driver slapped the reins.

"Step Clyde," he tugged, "Step Clyde. Let's go good horse. Step Clyde."

At the end of the first street, Shasta's eyes were heavy, and her head dropped onto Volt's shoulder. Street lights reflected off the Savannah River as she lay content in his arms. Volt was falling for her, and he knew it. It was less than a month into the relationship. "I may need to give it some time to see how she feels," he said with a low voice. "Reporting back to duty is going to be tough." Kissing her head, he shuffled his legs to make her more comfortable, relaxing alongside her.

II

Three Cottages at Hilton Head

Mickey continued to recover. George and Raquel agreed to take care of him while Volt and Terry, under Tipp's command, operated the rental boats. The guys scheduled a light half-day on the ocean as Tipp and Volt planned to meet Shasta and her friend, Nicole, at the dock.

"Hey, there are the ladies," yelled Tipp.

Volt unhooked the ropes, leaving one wrapped until they climbed aboard.

"Told you she'd be pretty," said Volt.

"You're right, she's adorable." Tipp removed his sunglasses. "With that tan, she must live outdoors."

"They brought food," whispered Volt. "Good food, I bet."

"Any friend of Shasta's is a friend of mine," Tipp remarked, reaching forward to greet Nicole. "Let's take these ladies to Hilton Head Island," he suggested. "Mickey has a few cottages about a half-hour north. What do you say?"

"Good idea," said Volt. "How 'bout it, ladies?"

"I told you he was a cutie," Shasta whispered in her friend's ear.

"Little bit of cloud cover, but no rain in sight," said the singer, stealing a kiss as Shasta gained her balance. "Tipp's taking us on a coastal tour."

"Let me help you with your bags," Tipp offered, placing Nicole's cooler under the seat. "This cooler is heavy. What did you bring, crab legs?"

"I packed us all lunch," Nicole said with a festive look.

Her southern drawl caught Tipp's attention, having a thing for southern ladies, and she was one to watch.

Nicole turned to Tipp. "I heard through the grapevine, you like turkey and cranberry sandwiches, sea salt chips, and cherry soda."

Tipp tilted his head and appreciated her thoughtfulness. "Listen, should I march to see your father about taking your hand, here and now?" he laughed.

Nicole looked over her dark sunglasses and winked.

"Cottages sound fun, Tipp." Nicole stretched out on the seat cushions, wiggling her toes and rubbing herself down with tanning lotion.

"The runway is clear for takeoff." Tipp checked his watch. "Please fasten your seatbelts, ladies, and Volt; this rocket ship is ready for lift-off," said Tipp, who throttled down the engine.

"Sit back and relax," said Nicole, winking at the captain. "Tipp is in control. Let's go to South Carolina."

Tipp headed north as Volt and the ladies slathered on sunscreen. The captain maneuvered the coastline like a pro. Mickey would have been proud of how his grandson approached the waves and read the landscape, which included Blackbeard's hideaway, where the Savannah River empties into the Atlantic Ocean. Tipp couldn't hear the conversation of his passengers due to the waves and the loud motor right behind him. Nicole joined Tipp and sat close.

"It's boring up there with no one to talk to," she said, approaching the wheel. "Hope you don't mind my company."

Her gentle personality was a reassuring trait after some of the other girls Tipp dated in college.

"So, where are you from?" Tipp asked, turning in her direction.

"Athens, Georgia."

"Cool college town, I've hung out there."

"I graduated from UGA, but I live in Savannah now. I design clothing. That's how I met Shasta; she models for my company."

"Wow!" He cocked his head in her direction. "Impressive," dropping his sunglasses to see her better. "Well, anyone who is a Bulldog gets to drive today. That's my secret rule." Tipp motioned for her to step closer to the wheel.

"Are you sure about me driving this big boat?"

"You will do fine."

Tipp placed her right behind the wheel and the other in front of him, noticing Nicole's bright pink fingernails that accented her bronze skin.

"I've never driven a boat before. Are you sure I can drive this thing?" Nicole placed her legs wide for balance and wrapped her hands around the wheel at ten and two like she was on her grandfather's tractor in Macon. Tipp pushed the throttle, and she nervously squealed.

"I'm right here," he assured her. "Don't panic. Alright, it's just like a car. Battery, fuel, accelerator, and a steering wheel. Push that button, now," he commanded.

HONK! HONK!

Shasta and Volt jumped and turned around in their seats.

"Sorry!" said Nicole, pointing at Tipp, who was laughing.

Nicole laughed hysterically, covering her mouth in embarrassment. Tipp's humorous personality kept them entertained. He throttled the handle and headed to familiar land.

"Daufuskie Island is on our left; a few famous people live there," Tipp shouted over the roar of twin engines. The Big Dog Café is our next stop. I'll fuel up at the marina. Mickey's cottages are not far from the water."

"Sounds good to me," responded Nicole.

Tipp backed off at the no-wake zone and cruised into the marina for fuel.

"I got the rope, Tipp," said Volt. "Be careful, stepping off the boat, ladies."

While fueling the boat, Tipp had an uneasy feeling as some beer-guzzling guys kept eyeing him. He headed inside to pay and rejoin his crew, who were grabbing a drink at the bar.

Tipp shifted to his right. Outside stood the two big guys who followed him from the marina.

"Volt, you got a minute?" asked Tipp, waving him to the exit. "Walk outside with me."

"Sure, what is it, captain?" Volt leaned toward Tipp as they stood on the sidewalk.

"Two guys followed me from the marina."

"Who are they?"

"Leaders of the Bull River Boys, Carter Cigar and Magnum Frisco, I believe."

Tipp tried to locate the guys behind the crepe myrtles and cedar trees, scanning the area a half dozen times for his enemies.

"I don't see them." Tipp looked down toward the marina one last time.

"Get away from us!" screamed Shasta.

"They're inside!" shouted Tipp, running to the door of the cafe.

"Found 'em." Volt loosened his shoulders for his enemies.

"You take the big one. I'll take the ugly, stocky guy with the big ponytail," said Tipp.

"Got it." Volt eyed his opponent.

Carter was a stocky guy with a ponytail, brown mustache, and pirate goatee. Magnum was the bigger guy with a large belly, barrel chest, and his face was covered in a dark beard. Both held long cigars in their teeth, wearing smug looks.

"You two want to step away from those ladies," said Tipp, inviting the thugs. "Meet us outside, will ya?"

Pow! A short older man fired his pistol, causing part of the ceiling tile to fall atop the long wooden bar. Nicole and Shasta screamed and dropped behind the bar.

"Won't be no fighting in my bar!" yelled the barkeeper. "Call the cops, Faye!"

The lady picked up the phone and dialed.

"That's ok. No cops today," Magnum shouted, snarling at the two men. "You ain't seen the last of the Bull River Boys, Mr. Starr and that lousy singer with you."

"Get the hell out!" said the owner. "You heard me!"

Magnum pointed his finger. "Your ass is mine, Tipp!"

Carter Cigar and Magnum Frisco exited the cafe backward with disappointed smirks, slamming the doors and cussing.

The bar owner shook his gun and pulled the women from behind the bar. "You ladies alright?" he asked while holstering his gun. "Guys? You alright over there?"

"We're fine," Tipp responded. "Everybody's alright."

"I'm glad you showed up, sir." Shasta smiled at the man, finding a seat beside Nicole at the end of the bar.

"Pour our friends a drink, Faye," said the old man.

"Give me a minute, Wayne."

146

She dropped the phone to speak. A large quiet lady with wavy brown hair who didn't smile much lined up four glasses in the center of the bar.

"I'll stick with sweet tea," said Tipp, who was beside Nicole. "If you don't mind?"

"What's your name, anyway?" questioned Volt.

"The name's Wayne Reynolds, and this is Faye. We have been married since Noah built his boat."

Volt slapped his shoulder. "Good to meet you, Mr. Reynolds."

"Call me Wayne," shaking the singer's hand. "Good to meet you, folks."

"We should call you, John Wayne." Shasta added, pointing at the owner.

They laughed and carried on. Faye snorted when she laughed. The group grinned and looked around the room to see if anyone else caught it. Her unusual laugh had broken the tension and brightened new friendships. Wayne took one last look around before he slipped his revolver back in the leather belt, a western-style holster that hung on a wooden post in the back office.

"I know who you are now, Tipp Starr. I remember you as a small boy, Mickey and Nedra used to bring you with them to Hilton Head. They'd belly up to the bar, and I'd line up soda in a shot glass. After four glasses of soda, you stumbled around like you were drunk. I heard about Mickey's fight with Carter from the guys at the yacht club." Wayne touched Tipp's shoulder. "How's Mickey doing, anyway?"

"He's too hard-headed to feel anything. I remember you as a kid." Tipp crushed his lemon and drained it in his tea. "The Son of the South is not 100 percent yet, but he's getting there."

"Last time I saw you, you were in Mickey's boat, wrapped inside a giant life jacket with popsicle legs hanging out. You weren't big as a pug-faced dog, either. What are y'all doing out this way?"

Tipp turned to Wayne and divulged Mickey's plan about the concert as a means to recoup some cashflow for his busted boats and lack of seafood.

"Wayne, say, you think Volt can headline for us?" asked Faye. "Ticket sales would more than pay for the big hole that bullet ripped in the ceiling."

Tipp seconded the plan just like Mickey taught him.

"Yeah, guess I will have to fix that hole." Wayne leaned on the bar, assessing the damage.

"I'd be glad to play at the Big Dog, Mr. Reynolds. Next week, maybe?"

"I'll have the hole patched by then. It's a deal! Put you on the calendar. Hear that, Faye?" Wayne stretched his hands above his head. "I'll get a great big banner printed. Saturday at 8 pm. Superstar Volt Hendricks at The Big Dog."

"Sounds great," said Volt. "I'll rock the crowd for you, Mr. Reynolds. I promise you that much."

"Hey, bring Mickey with you if the hard-ass feels up to his old friends from South Carolina," laughed Wayne.

"I'll try to get him to come if he's up to it."

Faye interrupted the conversation, "Sorry to hear about your grandmother, Tipp. She made the best peach pie in the South. Tell Mickey, in her honor, we use her cobbler recipe on Sundays. Sold a million slices, I bet."

"God bless you. Mickey will be glad to hear it." Tipp waved and headed out the door.

"See you Saturday with my guitar, Mr. John Wayne," yelled Volt through his hands. "Keep an eye on Mickey's boat for us."

"We will for sure," said Wayne.

"See ya next weekend," yelled Faye.

The group left the boat docked at The Big Dog and walked the short distance to Mickey's three summer cottages. The homes were nestled together at the end of a long pine thicket and down a private road with a trail of crushed seashells leading to each cottage. The furniture was a little outdated, but the homes were cozy. When Mickey bought the cottages, it was for his friends to get away from the world for a few days. Rustic yet private, they were nothing more than tiny houses.

Shasta smeared two fingers across the dusty kitchen table, causing Nicole to sneeze a few times. Tipp handed her an unopened tissue box for the next occurrence.

"Nedra may have been the last person to clean the cottage," said Tipp. The cottages were good weekenders that made Mickey a few dollars during the busy season.

Tipp enjoyed Nicole's turkey and cranberry sandwich, which tasted like an early Thanksgiving to him. Shasta had brought Volt an apple pie with cinnamon sprinkled on top. The pie was screaming for a scoop of vanilla ice cream and a tall glass of milk for the perfect accompaniment, but Mickey didn't have any groceries in the fridge. The top crust of the pie had softened and settled into the warm apples from the boat ride. It was delicious and as good as any restaurant frequented in the Lowcountry.

Volt talked of the scuffle between Magnum Frisco and Carter Cigar. They might be jumped again at the marina or while at the cottages. He stretched his legs and practiced his martial arts, partly hoping to impress Shasta but to also be prepared for a potential battle.

Shasta eyed Volt approvingly as she tidied up the cottage. She and Nicole wiped away the dust and swept the hardwood floors until they looked new. Tipp suggested they stay in the cottages after the concert, as well.

***

The group strolled the beach at Hilton Head, collecting a handful of shark teeth and stacking seashells in a red plastic pail that Nicole found at the first cottage. The tone shifted momentarily as a jellyfish had stung a little boy and made him cry. Shasta attended to him until his mother rushed down the beach to comfort him.

They soon headed back to the cottage to change their clothes. After returning to the marina, Tipp charted their course to arrive in Savannah before sundown. He couldn't wait to tell Mickey about seeing Wayne and Faye and to brag about how well the boat motors ran after Terry tuned up the engines. He was a master mechanic, but Mickey couldn't pay him what he was worth.

Tipp's romance blossomed with Nicole. He drove her back to her Savannah apartment, and like a true gentleman, he didn't press to go upstairs. Through the window, Nicole watched him leave. She fell against the door with a sigh of content. She told Shasta how she wanted a second date with the handsome man from Whitemarsh Island.

***

Shasta's parents returned from vacation, so Volt got to formally meet her mother and father at dinner. Mrs. McGregor recognized the attraction between Volt and Shasta as soon as they stepped inside their Whitemarsh home. Mr. McGregor was a lofty businessman who'd be hard to convince of Volt's good graces and overall intent with his daughter. Shasta's parents were impressed with both his kind nature and his incredible work ethic. Her father commented that it wasn't often that a man would work a second job on his vacation, and he brushed Volt's shoulder as he laughed.

Shasta asked Volt to sing for her family, and he obliged. The singer eagerly grabbed the guitar from his truck and sang one song, hardly turning his eyes from Shasta. Her mother could see the sparkle in her daughter's eyes as she sat beside her and sang along to the radio hit. The young lady was head over heels in love with the man at the top of the charts each week, The Great Volt Hendricks.

The evening passed quickly. Mr. McGregor had to rise early the next morning for an important meeting, so her mother followed him to bed. Shasta gave Volt a promising kiss as she gripped his hips and tightly held him against her body. He pressed her against the door and slowly kissed the side of her neck. Shasta gave him one final passionate kiss before urging him onto the front steps. He wanted to touch her more, but she refused his multiple offers.

Shasta was playing the game and playing it well. She was careful to not show how excited she got when he kissed her, but toyed with him just enough to keep him interested. Volt had no idea how hard it was for her to deny him. They talked about what their first romantic encounter would be like before their last kiss of the night. Shasta remembered his voice as she pulled the covers and shifted her legs and hips nervously with excitement before drifting off with a peaceful smile on her face.

12

Surprise Party

Raquel shared a wonderful idea with the ladies at brunch, about throwing Mickey a surprise 65th birthday party. Something small and intimate that would not be too overwhelming for him but would change the tone of recent events. The girls made a list and assigned each of the boys a job. George, Volt, and Terry shared the responsibilities and rushed to pick up party supplies and a few gifts. Raquel assembled hor d'oeuvres to get the group started as she thought about the night's menu.

Mickey healed reasonably well, considering his age and the severity of his concussion, but the two broken ribs continued to cause significant pain when he coughed. Tipp lured him out of the house to check on two boats Terry repaired. The insurance company refused to offer a reasonable settlement to replace the fleet, forcing Mickey to rent most of his boats and begin out of pocket repairs on a handful of salvageable watercraft.

Taking his mind off the litigious situation, the two examined the boats offloading at Bull River. Mickey clapped his hands when he saw that the boats were fishing again. The long-awaited repairs patched his ulcer and dismissed much of the tension he'd locked inside his body.

"Let's head back and celebrate," Tipp said, putting his arm around the old man.

"Now, this is a sign of good things to come," Mickey grunted and pulled himself into the truck. His rib pain appeared to have vanished.

"Thanks for taking care of business while I was laid up, Tipp."

"Anytime, ole man, anytime." Tipp nodded at his grandfather.

"Now, what shall I do about my Caddy?" asked Mickey, scratching his head.

Mickey's emotional attachment to his Caddy had him at a crossroads. He wasn't sure what he'd do with the car yet. The yellow convertible brought him and Nedra countless memories. Romantic weekends in Charleston and the week at Key Biscayne stood out the most. Long drives down country back roads with the top down and the radio up brought a smile to his face. But now, it was full of blood and charred with bad memories. Tipp followed Mickey as they walked to the door of Mickey's mansion.

"Surprise!" shouted a room full of friends, including Shasta's parents.

"What is this?" Mickey's eyes lit up like the fourth of July.

"We love you, Mickey!" shouted Shasta. "And we're glad you are feeling better."

George handed Mickey a champagne flute. Tipp tapped his glass of sweet tea for a great toast to his grandfather.

"We are about to toast the greatest man in Savannah, Mr. Mickey Starr, my grandfather," said Tipp. "He is an endless friend to us all. To Mickey Starr, the best fisherman in America and best friend on the planet!"

Everyone called out, "To Mickey!"

Mickey hugged his grandson for his speech.

"Say a few words," said Tipp.

"Let me thank the women because I know you ladies are responsible for this party," Mickey joked. "I have a lot of people to thank here tonight." Mickey glanced around the room. "First, Raquel and George for putting up with me while I was cooped up. Your ongoing care and dedication are priceless. I love you both," raising his hand to his heart. "I truly do."

"We love you too, Mickey." Raquel kissed his cheek and cried. George gripped his hand as everyone returned to their seats.

Mickey walked to the front of the room. "But I'm not finished." He looked for his mechanic. "Terry, thank you for getting my boats back on the water. I'm glad Volt talked you into leaving

North Carolina behind and helping us in Savannah. Come here, Big Guy," Mickey motioned to Terry.

"Mickey, you are the best," added Terry. "Thanks again for taking me in. I appreciate that."

"I want to thank the McGregor's for checking in on me every day. That peanut butter pie was superb," he smiled, pointing to Mrs. McGregor. "And Mr. McGregor, thank you for the fine imported cigars." Mickey winked at the two and armed the two thumbs up gesture. Everyone was having a good time. Mickey's friends were glad to see him active and smiling again.

"I love you two like my own children." Mickey tilted his glass in the direction of the McGregors.

"Awww," said Mrs. McGregor. "We love you too, Mickey."

"Love you, Mr. Starr," replied Mr. McGregor.

"Who's next? Shasta and Nicole. You two brought the most beautiful flowers I have ever seen to the hospital. Thank you for slipping the Irish coffee into my thermos, too. You are saints to put up with this motley crew," Mickey teased.

The crowd howled at Mickey's quick wit.

"I need a hug from you two sweet ladies. Love you, Shasta. Thank you so much, Nicole. I adore you girls."

"I love you, Mickey," returned Shasta leaving a lipstick smudge on his cheek.

"I don't know you that well," said Nicole. "But you are an easy man to love. You are a good man to these people," kissing his other cheek. "I'm here for you if you need me."

"You are a great lady for Tipp," said Mickey. "Tipp and Nicole, we need some grandkids around here."

"Slow down," Tipp said, kissing and hugging Nicole.

The two made a great couple, and Mickey could see the sparkle in his grandson's eyes. Nicole was new to the group but fit as if she had been there all along.

"I know I'm missing someone. Volt? Where'd you go?

Volt cleared his throat, and the tall man peered over the guests.

"Sitting at the bar, as always," Volt raised his glass.

Mickey continued, "I'm not sure if there's a better soldier in the country than Volt Hendricks or a better singer, either. I salute you, Volt, for being a solid example of a proper man. You are doing your due diligence in serving your country, you chased your dreams in the music industry, and as if there couldn't be anything more you could add to your list, you work your tail off on your leave just to help out friends. You're a stand-up kind of guy, and I'm honored to call you friend. We love you buddy. To Volt Hendricks." Everyone followed Mickey, raising their glass and shouting, "To Volt Hendricks!"

Volt waited for everyone to finish. He looked Mickey in the eye, offering him gratitude and standing atop his fireplace hearth beside him. Mickey's black eye was barely noticeable, and his Irish pale color had returned. He was back to his old self again. Volt shuffled his feet to the fireplace, under the centerpiece was a traditional area, where Mickey spoke to his guests. So, Volt did the same, replacing Mickey atop the hearth.

"I'd like to make a toast to my best friend, Mickey Starr." He cleared his throat and turned on a big smile. "Good friends are hard to find unless you know Mickey. When circumstances cause others to act heartless, Mickey opens his heart even wider. When folks are short on cash, Mickey opens his wallet." Volt spoke louder. "When folks are hungry, Mickey turns on the grill. When friends want to party, Mickey opens the bar and his home." Volt lifted his glass, shouting, "That's why we call Mickey Starr, southern royalty. He truly is the great 'Son of the South'."

"Thank you all," said Mickey. He walked over to his grandson. "Tipp, we have a game of pool we need to finish."

"Yes, we do."

Whistling from across the room, Mickey flagged his hand, and asked, "Terry, will you and Mr. McGregor like to join us for a game of pool?"

"Be glad to play you," accepted Terry.

"Rack 'em up," said Mr. McGregor. "I haven't played pool in years."

Mickey stamped his pool stick several times on the tile floor. "Might be a good time to place a wager with these guys, Tipp?"

Shasta's father, Rick, settled himself on a comfortable bar stool and watched the break.

Terry patted his unsettled teammate on the shoulder and said in his Carolina accent, "Me and Gregor, here, will take you two on the next game," reaching in his wallet. "Make it best of three."

George and Raquel prepared the meal and served beverages. After dinner, Volt and Shasta walked out to the river. The water was clear enough to see smallmouth bass swimming and a few sunfish dashing under the dock.

Shasta held Volt's strong hand as they leaned on the wooden railing that ran along the riverbank. A gentle wind whispered through the sage grass just enough to cool the evening air.

"You know you've impressed my parents," said Shasta. "They like you."

"I thought your mother might like me. She's sweet, but your father is a hard apple to peel," he added.

Her finger twirled in his palm.

"I'm happy with you. You're friendly and smart, talented, devastatingly handsome, but too many girls flock to you. That part is hard for me." Shasta shared why she was keeping her guard up.

"Well, guys do the same with you. You are a model for crying out loud!"

"The runway is my job," she replied, angling her sweet smile.

"The stage is mine," countered Volt.

Dropping bread on the water, Shasta cleaned her hands.

"We both knew this on day one."

His voice became elevated. "You knew I was a singer before we ever met."

"Now what?" she asked while sipping her wine and nervously kicking her leg.

"We accept this about each other or..." he looked directly into her eyes.

"Or what?" she snapped back, turning to him.

161

"Or we walk away and pretend this never happened. How do you feel?" Volt leaned in intimately.

She hooked the belt loops at his hips like she did at the beach and looked into his sapphire blue eyes. "I have a serious question for you."

"What's on your mind?" He brushed his hand across her neck.

"Volt, do you want us to happen, or do we just walk away? I'm serious. Be honest with me."

Volt let out a sigh as he turned toward the river in deep thought. He paused to form the right words for her. Shasta was growing frustrated in the delay of his answer.

"I'm right here," said Shasta, watching his reaction. "You need to address this." Her stern voice was new to him.

Volt replied in his deep tone. "I'm in because I think the things that bother you are minor. We enjoy one another, we have fun together. I think about you constantly and always want to be with you. I don't want to let that go."

Shasta was calmed by the sincerity she saw in his eyes and heard in his words. "I agree."

"I think the hard part is not our fans, the hard part will be matching up our work schedules so that we can spend time together after I report back to the Army."

"That's true." She picked the top off a cattail bush. "You are leaving so soon, and I worry about us being apart."

"I loved you the first time I saw you at Mickey's dinner," he confessed, touching her chin and wrapping her in his arms. "I am devoted to you, Shasta. I feel close to you."

"I don't want to get hurt, that's all." Tears fell from Shasta's eyes.

"When I give my word, I do it," Volt assured her as he wiped a tear from her cheek.

Satisfied with Volt's response, Shasta kissed him passionately. "There, sealed with a kiss. You can't back out now."

She teased as the two walked back into the house.

"Where is everyone?" Volt looked around at a nearly empty house. "Man, we were outside a long time."

"Your mother left right after dinner with a headache. I saw Tipp walk Nicole to her car, and Mickey went on up to bed," said George. "Not sure where Tipp is now. Your dad left when their pool game was over. He said he'll see you in the morning, Miss Shasta."

They would later find out Nicole left for Nashville, ending her relationship before it became serious.

"Thanks, George. Well, now what?" asked Shasta, turning to Volt.

"I can show you my room," said Volt, pulling her down the long hallway to where he rehearsed and slept.

Her heart skipped a beat, but keeping her cool, she replied, "Maybe I should go home." Deep inside, she wanted to go with him, so she followed. "Okay, I can stay for a few minutes, that's all."

Shasta scanned Volt's room, it had very little light from the outside. A long wooden dresser lined the wall, and his guitar stood alone in the corner. Volt turned on the radio and kept the volume low.

"Ah, James Taylor," said Volt, turning around. "He's a North Carolina boy, you know?"

"You are sweet," she touched his hand. "You know that. But if you hadn't said something, I would've walked away as if this never happened."

The two lovers embraced on the bed while listening to music. Shasta laid on her side with her back against Volt's body. She used his arm as a pillow to protect the shape and style of her hair. Volt's hand stroked her lower back. She was nervous, breathing hard. With her guard up, her body responded to his touch, but her mind was holding her back. Volt was careful not to move too quickly and spook her. He enjoyed the privacy and her company

164

but found her body difficult to resist. Chills covered her tanned skin as she arched her back and closed her eyes.

"I better go," she mumbled.

"It seems you want to stay." His arm slowly made its way under the back of her shirt. He slid his fingers gently across her smooth skin and unhooked her bra.

"I know I have to go now," she whispered but didn't remove his hand.

"Stay the night with me," he said, lifting her hair to kiss the back of her neck.

Unable to resist, Shasta turned to face Volt then placed her chest onto his, continuing to make out with him. Volt's hand moved along the outside of her breasts then across her thin hourglass shape.

She grabbed his hand, saying, "We better stop before this goes too far, and I decide to…"

"How far do you want to go?"

"We both know the answer to that, but it can't go that far. I'm sorry." She shook her head. "I should go now," she said, pulling away.

"I'll walk you home," Volt replied, disappointed. "The invitation still stands."

Shasta stood her ground and refused his offer, despite the difficulty.

The two walked hand in hand across the lawn to Shasta's house. Volt thought he said something wrong.

"Are you mad at me?" He stood with less confidence. "Did I do or say something that upset you?"

Shasta released his hand. "No, I'm just being smart about us. Don't think I don't want you because I do." With a quick peck on the cheek, Shasta ran from the lamppost to her front door.

"Goodnight!" Volt shouted from underneath the light. He wasn't able to get her out of his head. At the same time, Shasta twirled her long hair and thought about what would have happened had she not cut bait and left. She closed her eyes and imagined what she wanted to do with him. Restless and unable to sleep, Shasta walked through her backyard garden over analyzing Volt in such a frenzy. The smell of nature filled her senses as the strong fragrance of the garden somehow reminded her of wedding bouquets. The full moon lit the sky as she rested on the long brick wall. She hoped that the sound of the moving water would bring tranquility to her racing thoughts.

"Peaceful, isn't it?" a familiar voice asked.

"Volt?" her head turned to him. "What in the world are you doing out here?" She turned her body toward him. "You almost gave me a heart attack."

"I couldn't sleep either."

He was perched forty feet away, seated atop Mickey's flagstone steps. Shasta walked towards him. Reaching her hand for his and said, "Help me over the wall."

He lifted her down, spinning her around slowly like they were on the ballroom dance floor.

"Are you going to sweep me off my feet, or something?"

"I've already done that, I believe."

She giggled. "I'm sorry, I just, I mean, I..." Shasta wrapped her arms around Volt, pressing her head against his chest.

"Shhhhhh," comforted Volt.

Volt carried her slender frame from the backyard, and the two walked to the room he was using at Mickey's. He gently placed her on his bed and reclined back on a stack of pillows. Shasta knew she would have to pursue Volt earnestly. Her previous actions caused him to retreat physically. She apologized for all of the mixed signals earlier, stroking his chest. Volt grinned, touching her chin and running his hand behind her ear. The first button removed. Then the next. Shasta slipped her hand inside his shirt to his bare chest as the soft music played.

Volt grazed the top of her shoulders with his fingertips, moving her soft hair, and kissing her forehead. He had reservations about touching her intimately for fear of rejection. He moved slowly to test the waters. Volt rubbed her waistline. Her skin was smooth and warm to the touch and she became comfortable with him.

With a soft voice, she told him, "I love you."

"I love you too," he responded with certainty.

Volt's unbuttoned shirt now draped across the back of a wooden desk chair. She lifted her body from the bed just enough to remove her shirt and bra. Volt received the green light from her nod and smile. He pulled the crisp sheet over her body to keep her warm as he eased the rest of her clothing off, kissing her body softly as he undressed her. Then he quickly undressed. Volt descended his hand from her chin and crept back to her navel. To hide her nervousness, she made small circles on his back with her sharp nails. Her heart raced. She pressed against him slowly and moved in for a kiss.

Knock! Knock! a hard thump sounded on the outside of the door several times. "Mr. Volt!" shouted George. "Hurry, it's your brother. It sounds urgent, sir."

"Just a second, George." Volt reached for his pants, made sure Shasta was covered, and rushed to the door.

"Where's Terry?" Barefoot and without a shirt, Volt stepped into the hallway to hear George's story. "Where's my brother?"

"Tipp's bringing him inside."

Shasta got dressed once Volt met George in the hallway and soon joined the men.

Shasta and Volt ran outside. Terry's head was bleeding. Tipp and Volt pulled him from the truck through the mudroom and down the hall to the sofa.

"Terry, what happened?" asked Volt. "Who did this?"

"Carter and Magnum," said Tipp, pressing a clean shirt onto Terry's wound.

"What happened?" asked Shasta.

Volt helped walk his little brother to a small guest bathroom near the great room. Terry was slow to answer, as his head throbbed.

"After I paid for gas," moaned Terry, "Carter and Magnum jumped out from behind the station, clubbed the heck out of me and took off."

Volt grabbed a towel. "That's a bad cut."

Shasta stepped back, covering her mouth after seeing the pool of blood from the deep gash.

"Wake Mickey!" Tipp told George.

"We'll get Carter and Magnum for this crap," said Tipp, hitting the wall with his fist. "I should have been watching his back. It's my fault, Terry."

The wounded man raised his head, turning to Tipp, "Don't worry. I got in a few good body shots before they ran off. Carolina mosquitoes hit harder than those wimps."

Blood dripped from his head as he stopped his nose from bleeding. In the mirror, he watched as Volt tended to him.

"Here's a cold cloth," said his brother, wetting one of the guest towels. "Take a seat."

Mickey rushed into the guest room. "Make way, damn it!" grabbing his head. "Let me see him."

The old man opened a bottle of rubbing alcohol and dabbed the area with a dry hand towel hanging on the wall.

"George, bring me a low stool, please."

"Damn, that alcohol burns!" yelled Terry. "I need a drink, George, could you?"

George returned, handing Terry a beer. Mickey dressed the wounded man with the first aid kit.

"Good beer," said Terry. "Thanks, George."

Mickey examined his cuts. "Get him some ice."

"What are we going to do about these guys?" Volt turned to Mickey.

"First, we stay together," said Mickey. "No one goes out alone." Mickey continued, "That includes Shasta, George, and Raquel. All of us," he declared, pointing to each person.

The group moved into the den. Mickey paced the floor, searching for something of motivation as he often did in front of a crowd.

"Let's be cautious from here on out and help each other." Mickey stood tall in his black robe with his embroidered monogram above the left pocket. "Volt, the Hilton Head gig is coming up soon. I fear there will be trouble there." Mickey brushed his chest. "Damn those two dirty bastards!" The old man struck the fireplace. "I ran into Carter. Then Tipp and Volt, and now, Terry. Anyone could be next," warned Mickey. "Y'all need to be careful."

"Give me the go-ahead, Mickey." Volt volunteered. "I'll do whatever is needed."

"Well, what I want to do and what I should do, are two separate entities, right now. I want to take them out. Just totally wipe them off the map with my bare hands," he said, pacing around the hearth. "But I also know that it will be a temporary solution. God would want more from us than to get all fired up and ending up in prison, or worse. Besides, we're here to help one another, forgive one another and not much more."

Mickey's mention of God brought an uncomfortable silence to the room. Lifting the mood, Volt suggested, "We'll hit 'em then ask for forgiveness, right?" He jokingly planted his fist inside his large, opened hand.

Soul searching warmed Tipp's heart and to hear it from his grandfather for the first time especially brought a smile as he thought of his grandmother Nedra; she'd be proud.

"You're right, Mickey. We've got to help one another. If it wasn't for you, I'd still be an addict in the Blue Ridge Mountains," said Terry, who offered a hearty salute to the man.

"Yeah, if it wasn't for Mickey, my ass would be working at a drive-thru in Augusta or on a golf cart handing out beer and soda," George chimed in his honor.

"Well, I appreciate the sentiments, but we've all supported each other in some heartfelt way. And there will be ample opportunity to continue helping one another," stated Mickey.

"I wish you could make my head feel better," replied Terry, removing the ice pack from his head. His remarks lightened the mood, and the group laughed.

"I was hoping one of you might get the picture, Picasso. It's taken me a long time to get it, I mean really understand it, but life is best lived with a selfless heart and a faithful mind. When Nedra died, it broke my heart worse than any hurricane ever did," he put his fist over his chest. "But her death taught me the importance of investing more in people and less in possessions. I'm still learning the process, right Tipp?"

Mickey lowered his head to hide his watery eyes. His grandson lifted his head and let him finish his speech. Smiling from ear to ear about his grandfather's faith and how long it had taken to reach his heart.

"Nedra would be pleased, too." Tipp hugged him and wept.

***

Volt returned from walking Shasta home and seated himself at the kitchen table, resting his head in his hand. Mickey saw his friend through the wide glass doors. The old man thought he would check on the soldier.

"What are you still doing up, Mick?" asked Volt, rolling a shot glass in his hand at the kitchen table.

"Wasn't ready for bed yet, and I found my cigar instead," said Mickey. "Mind if I join you for a drink, soldier?"

"Nope. Go ahead," he slid the bottle across the table. "Have a shot. You bought it."

They laughed at each other.

"Some good stuff from Kentucky that George ordered," Mickey said, struggling to steady his pour.

Volt grabbed the bottle. "Here, he said," setting the glass down, "I got this one."

"Didn't know you liked whiskey?" Mickey questioned as he held the glass in his hand.

"Nobody likes whiskey, do they? It's more for medicinal purposes, I think."

The two laughed. Volt adjusted his chair, leaning toward Mickey.

"Why'd you get all spiritual on us tonight, preacher?"

"Well, I guess I feel like we all need a change, first of all, me." Mickey dodged the seriousness of the question. "Even an old man doesn't have all the answers to all the questions. I need to change a few things, I guess." He poured a shot this time and gritted his teeth.

"Neither do the Army chaplains."

"What I'm doing doesn't feel like it's working much," said Mickey, dropping his head. "Sometimes, I feel a reprieve from reality is needed."

"Amen to that," Volt added in support.

"What's eating at you, Volt?" He rested his cigar. "You got twins on the way or something?" joked Mickey.

"It's like we solve one problem, then another one pops up."

"You have no idea. Can I tell you something, and you keep it under your hat?"

"Of course, what's up, Mick?"

Mickey searched his heart. "Hadn't talked to anyone much, but..." he pulled his goatee and stared at the whiskey bottle. "I don't know how to say this, but I'm a little low." Mickey rested his elbows on the table and gripped the bottle firmly with both hands, appearing sullen.

"Low?" Volt leaned in. "Low on what?"

"Low on cash, Volt. Very low on cash."

"You're making it, aren't you? Just have to wait for the insurance claim to pay off, and you'll be better than ever, right?"

"I confess. The insurance paid a while back, but I was so far in the hole that I couldn't recoup. I'm trying to unload some of my car collection, but finding a buyer in such a short amount of time has been tough.

"Selling your cars?"

"Yeah, I admit, I waited too late to loosen my load because my greedy nature wanted to hang on to it all," Mickey spoke low, continuing to divulge his financial dilemma.

"What about your ranch in West Texas?"

"No rain. Bad year for that part of Texas." Mickey brushed the top of his crew cut with both hands. "Dry times out there, and it's not worth a penny amidst a drought. Tipp is the only one who is aware of money being tight, but even he doesn't know that the 'Son of the South' is a phony in financial ruin." Quickly changing the subject, Mickey asked, "Enough about me, what's got you sitting up drinking the bottom out of this whiskey bottle?"

The singer rubbed his stubbled face and closed his eyes, pressing his hands on the table. "I'm being deployed again." Volt made his whiskey disappear and wiped his mouth with the back of his hand.

"Where are you going this time?"

"Not sure yet."

"Iraq, I bet?" Mickey rubbed his hands together. "Media is sending journalists to the Middle East. Shasta doesn't know, does she?"

Volt shook his head.

"Nobody knows, not even Terry. Only you. It's hard to keep a woman when you're on another continent," confided Volt.

"Yes, but it can be done. I know. And it's worth the work. Dedication and loyalty are hard to find, so when you do find it, you better make sure you don't lose it," Mickey continued the lecture to the young man, being a long-distance relationship expert, who served in Korea. "It's not that hard, all you need are two people who genuinely love each other."

"I love her, Mickey."

"I know you do, son." He toasted him. "I know you do."

13

Innocence

The Volt Hendricks' concert on Hilton Head Island proved to be one of the best shows of the decade. While the show was a big hit, Mickey's mind was spinning about getting more boats in the water from the concert revenue. He needed income to climb out of suffocating amounts of debt. On top of that, Mickey was obsessed with nailing the Bull River Boys for stealing boats and causing so much trouble with him and his friends. Carter and Magnum needed to be taken down for what they'd done to Terry and himself. Mickey was plagued with wondering who the next victim would be and when it might happen.

After the concert, Mickey witnessed a change in demeanor with Volt. Perhaps, his actions were due to their conversation about deployment. A week from being shipped off to the Persian Gulf would shake anybody, Mickey thought. More than that, Volt's zeal was missing. His charming smile and charisma faded as he signed autographs and met with fans. Volt's actions appeared robotic; his mind was distracted.

"Volt, you got a minute?" asked Mickey.

"Of course."

The two walked down to the water and looked out over the Intercoastal Waterway. Mickey stopped to admire the speed boats docked beside each other.

"How's it going on the inside?" he asked, looking at the singer. "You alright? I sense something is wrong with you."

"I'm fine." Volt denied his emotions.

"Fine is not what you are today. I'm here for you, right?"

Mickey patted his shoulder and walked back to the crowd.

"Yeah. Wait! Mickey, you are too damn smart. Alright, you got me," Volt admitted. "Okay, it's Shasta." Volt continued to stare across the water at the boats crossing in the distance.

"You have fallen for her." Mickey rotated his watch around his wrist. "And she's, of course, fallen for you." Mickey stood, resting his arms on a docked boat. "I know her. Well, what?" he asked, staring at the soldier. "What's your plan?" he piped up, "Make sure you are thinking with the right head, Romeo?"

Volt laughed and tried to relax. "I'm thinking with my heart. She's something special," he said in a low voice. Volt stretched out on the bench and took a deep breath.

"I'll leave you with your thoughts. Have a good night. See you in the morning," said Mickey, taking the path back to his cottage. Volt remained standing by the water for a few minutes and then returned to the line of people waiting on him.

Later, Volt knocked on Shasta's cottage door. She gave her makeup one last look in an over-the-door mirror and checked her long eyelashes. Rushing to the door, she brushed her fingers through her hair, anticipating Volt was on the other side. With one last adjustment to her hair, she tucked her long bangs behind her right ear, smiled and answered the door.

Volt stepped down on the ground under the yellow porch light and waited. He held a bottle of Capri, the type of red wine Shasta mentioned she wanted for their particular late-night date. The hand-selected barrel brand was shipped by Mickey into Hilton Head from the Bay of Naples in southern Italy. The other hand held a large straw basket of herbed cheese and assorted crackers that she favored.

The cottage door opened, and with one look at her radiant smile, he almost forgot about his pressing conversation earlier.

"Thought you'd gotten lost or attacked by an alligator or something," Shasta teased as she motioned for him to come inside.

He laughed and moved to the first step.

"I'm not coming inside tonight. Exhausting day," admitted Volt. "I just wanted to bring you a gift to let you know I was thinking of you and see that radiant smile."

"Come on in," insisted Shasta.

"You look unbelievable, by the way," complimenting her while he scanned how attractive she was in blue jeans.

Shasta spun around in a circle like a dancer.

"Wow, a gift," Shasta squealed with delight as she opened the bag. "You remembered the wine I like." She kissed him and made her way to the kitchen in search of glasses and an opener.

Volt picked her up and hugged her as if he hadn't seen her in months. When her feet were firmly planted on the floor, Shasta pressed her finger on his lips then moved him to the sofa for a kiss. He could taste wine on her lips, and could tell she was more flirtatious than he'd seen before. Her head tilted back as he descended from her ears to her neckline with his hands and lips, sliding further down her body. Her heart beat wildly, and she closed her eyes, enjoying his touch.

The scent of cinnamon filled the air from a candle burning on a nearby end table. The two separated long enough to peruse the snacks in the basket, playfully feeding one another.

"Great concert," she said, turning up the glass of wine. "You were fantastic!"

"It could have been better, but I'm glad you enjoyed it. Listen, uh, I'm sorry to cut this night so short, but I'm pretty exhausted. I'm gonna sack out if I sit here any longer."

"Well, you can take a cat nap here if you like."

"Been a long day. I just wanted to stop by and bring you a bite to eat, and get a goodnight kiss before I leave."

"You can have more than a goodnight kiss," Shasta offered coyly.

Volt slowly stood and stretched. He yawned loudly. As if his yawn was contagious, Shasta began to yawn, too. "I don't mean to keep you," Volt added as he inched toward the door.

Shasta, clearly feeling rejected, opened the door to initiate Volt's exit. Walking out, Volt noticed it had begun to rain.

"Ugh," he shouted. "It's pouring."

"Guess you better hurry home," Shasta shot back, slamming the door.

With a drenched head and shirt, Volt made his way back to Mickey's cottage and knocked.

"Just a minute! Be right there," Mickey called out. "What are you doing in the rain?" Volt stepped inside and removed his dirty shoes. Mickey grabbed a towel. "Here, dry yourself off."

Volt rubbed his long face. "Can I crash on your sofa?"

"She's all yours." Mickey sat back down at the table with his newspaper.

He fetched a towel and robe for his guest. Volt towel-dried his face and neck then quickly returned with an armload of clothes to throw in the dryer. The two sat at the kitchen table as the clothes whirled round and round. Volt leaned back on the chair as Mickey tended to Mexican chips and salsa. He opened himself a cold beer, and with a mouth full of tortilla chips, asked, "Where's Shasta? I didn't expect to see you until after breakfast." The old man stroked his goatee and leaned forward to listen.

"I'm not sure I did the right thing tonight," confessed Volt.

"Did you sleep with her?"

"Nope." He dropped his head. "Told her I was tired from the concert."

"Then, you did the right thing. Was she mad?"

"I think she was disappointed but didn't say too much," said Volt. "Not that I would have heard it over the slamming of the door anyways."

"She got mad as hell, I bet?"

"Damn right," Volt answered, taking a drink.

"You made a noble gesture, son," bragged Mickey.

"I'm noble and alone tonight, as you can see," Volt threw his arms in the air.

"I know you are kicking yourself right now, but you won't regret it."

"I may not be as noble next time," replied Volt, disappointed.

***

Meanwhile, Shasta finished another glass of wine and sat solemnly in the wake of Volt's rejection. She was confused and emotional from his actions. Angry and hurt, she went to bed, alone.

***

Eager to smooth things over with Shasta, Volt awoke early.

Knock. Knock. He waited patiently. He cracked the door slightly and called out, "Shasta?" Volt observed a folded note purposely placed on the floor near the door. The note had his name written in large letters. Grabbing the note from the floor, he unfolded the paper.

Dear Volt,

After you left last night, my heart was broken. My feelings were hurt, and I can't understand why you are toying with me. If I'm not good enough for you, then stay away. I will be just fine without you.

Shasta

Volt closed the door and sat on the steps. He regretted doing what he thought was the right thing. Being easy with girls was a sore spot with Shasta, so to offset his 'typical musician lifestyle,' he insisted on proving that his intentions were relationship worthy. Failed attempt. Failed coercion. Volt's determination to keep his word and her virtue, somehow, became misconstrued. He didn't blame her for being frustrated by his mixed signals. First, he showed up bearing gifts, and just as quickly, he rushed out the door.

"Bolting Volt, that's gonna be what she calls me if she ever calls me again," he pouted.

The return trip to Savannah seemed much longer and quieter. Mickey probed Volt about what was bothering him. He spoke about his pending deployment but failed to mention the note from Shasta.

14

Guess Who?

Volt didn't have an appetite for Raquel's famous breakfast crepes. Instead, he took his thoughts and his guitar down by the water. Like a lost puppy, Volt didn't know what to do next. He strummed, sang a little, and secretly hoped Shasta would hear him next door and come out to join him. Disappointed, Volt returned to the house to find Mickey cleaning his pipe. Tipp and Terry were doing what they do best... eating.

"What's wrong, big brother?"

"What do you think?"

"He's just too damn noble for his own good," Mickey offered while boxing up his pipe collection.

Terry was clueless about what transpired after the concert. He'd elected to stay behind to repair one of Mickey's boat engines. The old man signaled Terry to discourage additional questions.

Mickey chimed in, "I have an idea," he dropped his fork and motioned to his grandson. "Tipp, take this soldier out on the town tonight. You boys pick out a car from the garage and cruise around."

"Stellar idea, Gramps," Tipp raised his hands in excitement. "Terry, you going?"

Terry was a wild man, who'd served time in prison. While he still had hell-raising tendencies, he was good at his core. Excited about a night on the town after tinkering with engines all weekend. "You know I'm in," hollered Terry.

"I appreciate the sentiment Mickey, but I'm not sure I'm up for it," Volt contemplated. "Had a rough breakup with Shasta last night."

Terry stopped chewing and rinsed his mouth with juice. "Hate to hear the news. Dad would've liked her."

"Me too, but I messed up-- another short-lived relationship. That's just my M.O." Volt picked at his plate. "I think I'll just stay in tonight. I can watch some football with Mickey and George, right, Mick?"

"Wrong," Mickey demanded. "Listen up, my friend. Tipp will drive y'all in the Victoria."

"The Victoria?" asked Tipp. "That '33 Ford will turn a quarter-mile in ten seconds flat. Are you sure?" Tipp surveyed his grandfather's face for certainty. The old man shook hands with his friends and hugged his grandson. As he handed Tipp the key, he saluted Volt and Terry from the doorway of the game room.

Later that day, George opened the bay and parked the car on the wet pavement after the rain passed. Two sharp-looking guys stood dressed to impress. From the second-floor hallway window, Mickey looked down at his favorite guests of all-time. Volt started the '33 Victoria and then climbed into the backseat as the motor thundered, and the neighbors walked across the lawn to see the car. Tipp rested his hand on his grandfather's shoulder before joining the two men. "Grandpa, you don't let anyone borrow your collection."

"No, I've never done it before, and it may not ever happen again." The old man joked as he wiped his mustache.

"Are you dying?"

"No." Mickey chuckled at his words. "No, Tipp. It's just that certain things are not a priority anymore."

Mickey knew he'd changed. He wasn't sure what caused his transformation, but he was enjoying the acclimation of having considerably less.

He and Tipp headed down to join the men. Tipp took the wheel and they headed out, leaving a trail of smoke and a line of marks on the driveway. The old man shouted through his hands, "Quit spinning my wheels!"

"I told him to do it," George admitted, slapping his leg, and jumping around. "It's all my fault, I knew you'd have a cow when the smoke rolled."

"You're all a bunch of knuckleheads," said Mickey, shaking his head. "George, you should have gone with them, they're gonna need help with the ladies." Mickey patted George on the back as they stood in the doorway.

"We are like brothers," said Mickey. "I'm the only Irish brother you have. Treasure of a man you are to the family, George," Mickey spoke in a faux Irish brogue.

***

Tipp and the guys hopped a few pubs enjoying Savannah's seafood, live music, and taking in the town, for them it was a great getaway.

"Ready gentlemen?" Tipp visually scanned the area.

"You bet," said the singer.

Tipp stopped to gas up, and Volt ran inside to pay the clerk and grab a soda from the station. Tipp checked his hair in the mirror. "The tank is full, boys, where to?"

"Nice of Mickey to let us take the car," said Terry.

"Yeah, it's kind of bittersweet. He just has too many things holding down his wallet," Tipp said, rubbing his head in frustration.

Volt and Terry eyed one another.

"Tipp, maybe we should call it a night," said Terry, looking down with a sense of shame. "I think me and Volt have worn out our welcome at Mickey's."

"No, no, no! That's not what I meant. You know what I'm talking about," said Tipp, trying to explain. "I mean, the storm knocked him completely out of business for a while. The concert proceeds saved him, literally."

"Glad to help," said Volt.

"He will never fully recoup the storm's loss, but thanks to some good friends, he's gonna make it. He's not making a killing but making a living and keeping people on the payroll," disclosed Tipp. He fears that the crew won't be able to provide for their families. Let's not talk about this anymore." Tipp checked his speed. Terry quickly changed the subject.

"Let's pull in at this place with the flashing neon lights," suggested Terry.

"Moon River Blues?" asked Tipp. "Yeah, they're famous for two things."

"What's that?" asked Terry. "I'm dying to know them both."

"I see one of them standing in line," Volt leaned forward.

"This place is a Saturday Night Special," said Tipp, scanning the area. "Known for snooty college ladies and hot beer."

"Wait! What?" asked Terry.

"I'm just kidding," said Tipp, easing their minds. "This is a great place."

The group entered with Terry barely clearing the door before chatting with a redheaded divorcee who was hell-bent on making her ex-husband jealous.

Several folks recognized Volt, but Terry was good at keeping people at bay so they could have a good time. A nice waitress latched onto Terry's arm. "Is Volt Hendrick's your brother?" The girl asked.

"Sometimes," winked Terry.

A waitress approached. "Follow me to your table."

The trio followed the young lady and was seated at a spacious tabletop near the stage.

"Are you singing tonight?"

"Not tonight," Volt answered the waitress. "Just here for the beer."

Volt hammered down a beer. The owner heard he was in the building and asked him to sing a few songs. Hesitantly he agreed after telling the waitress no, he reconsidered.

"Did you see those baby blue eyes?" asked Tipp, turning his body for a second look.

"No," said Terry. "Didn't pay attention to her eyes, never looked up that far."

The place was packed, and as with every bar, the girls seemed to outnumber the guys. Tipp ordered a soda and held onto the keys. Terry ordered a beer while Volt danced with a cute blonde and returned to his seat. Two soft hands covered Volt's eyes as a familiar voice asked, "Guess who? I'll give you two guesses."

"I'll only need one," Volt assured her. "I recognize the perfume."

"You better be right," warned the lady.

"Brandi with an i," said Volt.

She dropped her hands and fell in his lap. "Lucky guess," said Brandi, touching his nose. It's good to see you again."

"Uh, yep, been a long time, I guess." Volt rolled his eyes.

"Too long, Volt." She winked and wrapped her arms around his neck. "We should pick up where we left off before I moved to Dallas?"

"So, how's Texas, anyways?"

"Why Volt Hendricks, if I didn't know better, I'd think I was making you nervous," bragged Brandi. "It's hot, but I miss it. I miss being hot." Brandi continued toying with Volt.

"What are you doing in town?" Volt ignored her flirtatious language, struggling to keep the conversation straight.

"I'll be here until the first of the year," said Brandi. "You know how the holidays bring me back to Georgia."

"That sounds fun," Volt added half-heartedly. "Well, it's good to see you," turning his body away from her, hoping she would disappear.

Brandi helped herself to a seat at the table. "How's Mickey doing, Tipp?"

"Hardheaded as ever." Tipp grinned, looking around the room. "You know Mickey, full blast and ready for anything."

"How's Beth?"

"She and I broke it off," he answered, slightly dropping his head. "Last I heard she was back with her old boyfriend, but not sure."

Volt flagged down the waitress. "Three beers, one soda, please."

She nodded. "Anything for you, sweetheart?"

Brandi mocked the lady. "Anything for you, sweetheart?" she said sarcastically while twisting her hair and smacking her lips.

Finding her next disinterested victim, Brandi says, "Terry, how are you?"

"I'm good." Wanting to stir the pot, Terry added, "I have a question, though." Terry grabbed his chest and burped. "Excuse me. Sorry about that. But why did you go and break my brother's heart last year?"

The men all busted a gut laughing.

Volt waved him off. "Terry!"

Brandi inspected Volt's blank stare. "Did I break your big ole heart?" She puckered her lips and blew a kiss. "I didn't realize I was a heartbreaker."

Terry added, "After you left him, Volt had to visit the cardiac unit."

Tipp nearly spit his soda across the room.

"Brother, you need to be a comedian," commented Volt, glaring at Terry, and squinting.

A slow ballad began to play in the background. Brandi scooted closer to Volt and rubbed his thigh, whispering, "Let's dance."

She pulled Volt to the dance floor. A round of applause echoed in the room as Brandi and Volt stared into each other's eyes. Volt knew the crowd was watching, and for fear of looking like an ass and ending up in the papers, he played along. Her hazel eyes kept him locked as they spun around like an old vinyl record. Just as the song was ending, Brandi kissed him, and Volt responded. Leaving the dance floor, he pulled her hair back away from her face and initiated a tender peck on the cheek. Playing up the audience, Volt slapped hands with the guys on his path back to the table.

"You guys ready?" Tipp scanned the table. "It's about midnight."

"Will you guys turn into pumpkins or something?" Brandi bayed at them.

Terry and Volt shook their heads.

"Late?" said Terry. "We just got here."

"What do you think, Volt?" Tipp observed the couple kissing again.

"Just a minute," he was putting his hand on her lower back.

"Deacon Tipp, here, has a Sunday ritual," said Terry.

"I didn't know you were a minister, too, Tipp," said Brandi, nodding over the waitress. "I'll have another light beer, please."

"He's not." Volt eyed Tipp. "But he's a good man of faith, though."

Brandi responded with, "We all believe in Sunday confession, don't we?"

The men laughed.

"I guess it is getting late." Volt checked his wristwatch.

"I have an idea." Brandi touched her nose, winking at Volt. "Let's go back to Tipp's place and finish the night."

"I'm game." Terry leaned back in his seat.

"I'm waiting for the good idea part," Tipp said, shaking his head.

Brandi replied with a big smile, "I have two sorority sisters at the far table who would love to hang out, Tipp."

"Two nice-looking ladies?" Terry questioned Brandi.

"I'll settle the tab. This one is on Tipp Starr."

Volt grabbed his arm. "No. This one's on me. You've been good to me and my brother, I'll cash us out."

"Tipp, lead the way." Volt slapped Tipp's shoulder.

Brandi returned. "This is Catherine and Hadley."

The group exchanged pleasantries. Catherine was a small-framed lady, with sandy blonde hair and a cute subtle smile. Hadley was taller and the more talkative one in the group. Hadley took to Tipp right away, Terry escorted Catherine and opened the car door for her. Brandi and Volt hailed a taxi.

***

Tipp had a great place in the higher end of Savannah. It was left unattended much of the time as he worked and looked out for Mickey's. Tipp's house was a Depression-era constructed home with climbing green ivy creeping up the bricked front. It looked well-manicured for a single man.

"Beautiful home, Tipp," bragged Hadley.

"Do you have a family?" she asked, cautiously. "Married?"

"Nope, just me."

"This giant house and it's just you?" looking up at the tall ceiling. "Holy cow! Where do you work, and are they hiring?"

"Ha!" Tipp grabbed his stomach and laughed, "My grandfather helped me get this place."

"Who's your grandfather?"

"Mickey Starr."

"Your grandfather is millionaire Mickey!" She grabbed Tipp's arm in excitement. "Are you serious? I had no idea."

Confused by her excitement, Tipp asked, "Why?"

"You are not going to believe this, but my grandmother still has a huge crush on your grandfather from high school."

"Bethesda Academy?"

"Tell Mickey Starr that my grandmother is Rita Sampson."

"Rita Sampson. Okay. I'll tell him when I see him tomorrow for Sunday dinner."

"She gets all excited when she sees his logo. She goes on and on about his chiseled face and sky-blue eyes," touching Tipp's arm. "Must be where you get those rugged good looks, huh?"

"I'm a much younger version," Tipp chuckled.

Tipp was relieved to know they had a connection and she wasn't a lady who was merely financially motivated to be with him.

Hadley and Tipp walked around the garden.

"That's sweet." Tipp flashed his teeth with a big grin. "A forty-year-old crush. Now that's commitment!"

Tipp gestured to the back entrance, opening the door for her.

Hadley stepped inside. "Show me the way."

"Kitchen to the right. Living room to the left. The bathroom is under the stairwell," said Tipp. "Would you like a beer?"

"No. Don't drink. Soda will work. Diet, please, if you have it."

"My kind of lady." Tipp eyed her. "I have plenty of soda."

"I love the older style homes," she continued the conversation.

"Hope you didn't mind," said Volt. "We made ourselves at home."

"Of course, please make yourselves at home. Enjoy."

"Is everyone staying the night?" Tipp questioned, scanning the crowd. "I have plenty of room. Hadley?"

"Where's my room?" answered his friend. "I'll stay."

"Hell yeah, I'm stayin'," Terry yelled after he gunned a beer and caught his breath.

"Catherine, you in?" asked Terry. She nodded.

"Appreciate the southern hospitality, Tipp," mentioned Brandi. "Check me off for a room, as well. Volt might be afraid of the dark." She had a knack for making people have fun.

"More beers are in the fridge, remote control on the table, and there are snacks in the pantry."

Tipp and Hadley headed upstairs first. The two shared a friendly kiss before parting to separate rooms for the night. More of the group slowly detached and made their way to a resting place for the night. Volt and Brandi cuddled on the couch, watching television for a bit before heading up to their room.

The following morning, Catherine revealed to Hadley the wild morning she had with Terry in the shower. The two giggled about it in the hallway. Downstairs, Tipp prepared pancakes and sausage.

"Something smells good," said Volt. "Tipp, you can cook, too? Wow! You're a regular renaissance man, aren't you?"

Terry and Catherine grinned at each other across the table, each reminiscing their rendezvous. Volt pulled out a chair at the table for Brandi, where he received a soft kiss for his kindness.

"Last night was fun," said Tipp, holding Hadley's hand. "We should do it again sometime." She was a breath of fresh air and made them all laugh. Hadley was interested in Tipp but wasn't sure if the feeling was reciprocated. Still, she was hopeful.

15

Let's Talk

Mickey accepted the indisputable fact that while he was slowly dredging his way back from near financial ruin, he knew the empire he once built, would likely never recover. And on most days, he was okay with that.

The dark clouds had parted by the time Tipp rolled the loud classic car back in the driveway. Fall was moving in, and George and Raquel were beginning to decorate the house accordingly. As Tipp finished parking the car, he noticed a truck in the driveway he didn't recognize. In the scope of his vision, just beyond the green hedges, a clean-shaven, tall framed man closed the door to the truck, and waved when he exited. Tipp felt the man's face was familiar, but he couldn't place how the two had met.

As Tipp stared at the man, Volt commented on his truck.

"Nice truck. '55, right?" asked Volt.

"Sure is a sweet ride," said Terry, turning to see the truck.

"So, who got the most numbers last night?" Mickey joked with the guys.

"You boys head on in for some football," said Mickey, with a cup of coffee in his hand. "Meet you inside."

"Be there in a few," added Tipp as Mickey helped guide the car back into the garage. "Who was that man in the black truck?"

"Our friend from the pier."

Tipp tilted his head and pictured the man's face.

"I remember, but do I know him?"

"Grady Johnson, the man with the note in his pocket at the beach last month."

"Yeah. Yeah. Yeah," said Tipp with a curious look. "What was he doing here?" Tipp squinted with curiosity. "What did he need?"

"It was about the note at the beach."

"What was on the note?" asked Tipp. "Remind me."

"I wrote, 'It's me, Mickey Starr. Let's talk."

Tipp was lost. "I don't get it. Why'd you write that?"

"Park yourself." Mickey patted a seat signaling Tipp to sit nearby. "Grady is three years older than me. We went to high school together and played on the same team. A couple of guys didn't like that I was pretty good at basketball and was just a freshman in '44."

"You're still a great point guard," Tipp reminded him.

"Well, we got challenged to a game. Grady and I accepted. We wagered money on it."

"Did you beat them with your jump shot?"

Mickey stood using his hands to demonstrate. "Well, we were down by one. Grady passed the ball back to me on the outside. I faked but didn't have a good shot. So, I passed it to Grady on the inside. He turned and shot. The ball bounced around the rim a few times before finally dropping in."

"You won?"

"Hell yeah, we won," strutted the old man. "But back in those days, even if you won, you'd still have a fight on your hands."

"What happened? Did you fight?"

"Unfortunately, Grady has the gift of gab. He started talking crap and fired off at the mouth. They got even more pissed off and then started in on me."

Tipp piped up. "I would have given anything to have seen it."

"No, you wouldn't have wanted to see this. Trust me."

Mickey turned pale white.

"Why is that?" asked Tipp. "You lost the fight?"

"As Grady got close to the taller guy, the shorter one knifed him in the side before I could get to him."

"Stabbed him?" Tipp felt deep compassion for the so-called bum.

"His eyes caught mine. I saw his face just freeze. He never made a sound. Blood started to drip through his clothes, and down his side. The guys ran off. Grady just closed his eyes. He was in a lot of pain."

"What'd you do?"

"I looked around for help. Called out, but no one came to help us."

"That was bad news." Tipp leaned in as the story unfolded.

"I found a wheelbarrow in a small garden, pushed him to his step dad's gas station, a few blocks away. They rushed Grady to the emergency room. A pool of blood remained in the wheelbarrow after we loaded him in the car. I don't know how he recovered, but he did."

"You saved his life?"

"Well, I don't know. He later thanked me for it. So, he's convinced I did, I guess." Mickey turned and looked off. "After high school, he shipped out to the Navy, and I didn't see him but a time or two after that."

Tipp scooted to the edge of the bench anticipating more of the story. He suspected his grandfather had more to tell.

"I bumped into Grady; we chatted a bit. I had a date with your grandma planned." Mickey laughed heartily. "I didn't have a dime to my flippin' name." Grady said, 'Your date is on me.' Here's a small token for saving my life." He handed me a few bucks.

I said to him in return, 'You would have done the same for me.' We shook hands and parted ways."

"What a good friend."

"Grady Johnson stuffed my empty wallet with the greenest ten-dollar bill I'd ever seen. That was the money I took her out on the town with. We had the night of our lives." Mickey chuckled. "The best part was," he pointed out, "her parents thought I had lots of money after she'd told them I had spent ten dollars on her."

They both leaned back on the bench howling.

"Just ten dollars?"

"That would be like a hundred dollars now, Tipp."

"Wow." Tipp grinned. "You treated her right then, didn't you?"

Mickey nodded. "I did." He paced with his hands in his pockets.

"I proposed that weekend."

"What's that have to do with the note you left in his pocket?"

"Grady and I hadn't kept in touch much over the years. He lost his wife to cancer a few years back, and we became closer friends again. His sister had to move in with him to help him get his mind straight. He had a thriving career in real estate, and this year, thank God, he wanted to hunt on my Texas ranch outside Amarillo."

"I still don't get it." Tipp brushed his hand over his chin. "What's that have to do with the note, though?"

"Here's the good part, Tipp. He came to talk. Last week, he made a quick sale on the ranch in West Texas. Got a real good price, too. Saved me, financially speaking. I've been trying to get rid of a few things to keep us afloat, not expecting the ranch deal to come through so well and so quickly." Mickey handed Tipp a hundred dollars from his money, grinning with the debt relief coming to fruition.

Tipp high fived his grandfather and lifted both hands to the heavens and yelled. "My prayers have been answered! That's wonderful news! Thank God for that blessing. He was the man with the message, alright. He's proof that you can't count people out."

"It's good news." Mickey took a cloth from his garage and dusted the mirrors on the truck. "Real good news." Mickey breathed a sigh of relief.

"Yeah, we can get more boats repaired, more boats on the water, more people back to work, more money put back in the bank."

Tipp sat on the bench. "That's great!"

"Tipp, I bought a farm in Savannah."

"What do you need with a farm in Savannah? We're fishermen! Not farmers! Fishing is our family legacy."

"It's a good place, and you've seen it."

"You're up to your eyeballs in debt and having to call in favors for friends, and then you went and bought a damn farm? What has gotten into you, Grandpa?" Tipp slammed his fist against the bench several times. "Besides, you already own a place in Savannah."

Mickey carefully gathered his words.

"The farm I bought was the Tobacco Barn."

"You did what?" Tipp paced over beside him. "This makes no sense. Is this a joke? I don't get it?"

Mickey stood face to face with Tipp. "Grady Johnson is my half brother. Years ago, your grandma sold the barn to him so that we could grow the fishing business, double our fleet. Grady held on to it, assuming I would buy it back when fishing really took off. That's why we never shared that with you all.

"You should have told me."

"Time went on, we thought less and less about the barn, it got pushed aside and forgotten. Grady was kind enough to give us full access to the place, and I think, in the long run, that's what postponed us getting it back. When Nedra was in the hospital, she made me promise to get her barn back. Grady is a great guy. So incredibly generous."

"This is a lot to take in. Fishing and a farm." Tipp rubbed his forehead in dismay. "I don't get it. You desperately need money. You get the money. And then you turn around and spend it right back."

"I got a good deal on the Tobacco Barn," Mickey nodded.

"Got a good deal? Grandpa, are you listening to the words you are saying?" Tipp started to sweat, and Mickey gave him the cloth.

His grandfather had years of memories and kept his promise to Nedra even though Tipp looked at the world through the narrow lens of transactions, not from his grandmother's last request or even Mickey's side of the story. Tipp began to repeat the same questions over when Mickey interrupted.

"I repurchased the barn for $10.00. I'm only out ten bucks."

"Wait, what?" Tipp waited for him to explain.

"He only charged me ten dollars, which was a true cash debt I owed him on the first date with your grandmother. But Grady changed the name on the deed in honor of Nedra."

"So, we're good, right?"

Tipp turned to his grandfather. "Financially, at least?"

"Umm," Mickey hesitated. "It's not that easy. I guess life never is. But Carter Cigar is Grady's son." Mickey's words were deafening. "The grudge runs deep."

"Tomorrow, Grady is going with me to check out the place and take a look around. You are welcome to come along if you like?" Mickey lifted his head and puffed on a cigar as he lit it. He avoided looking at Tipp.

"I have a date with Hadley tomorrow," said Tipp. "I can't go. I'm sorry."

"That's fine. Grady and I will make the trip."

***

The next morning, a baby blue sky blanketed the coastal community. Mickey viewed the Wilmington River from his back deck and sipped coffee while reading the newspaper. The positive stroke of luck changed Mickey. It was like some sort of spiritual awakening welling up inside. After some deep, gritty soul searching, he concluded that Grady threaded this newfound inspiration through his heart, and he felt, with confidence, that the Lord sent Grady to help him recover.

Grady pulled up in his '55 truck. Mickey waited in the driveway, sporting the flat hat that made him a recognizable figure in the

South. He hardly recognized Grady in his new sport coat, clean-shaven, and surprisingly sober. Soon, the two brothers were en route to Tobacco Road.

Upon their arrival, Grady apologized for not keeping up the property and letting it run down. Mickey wasn't upset about the wear and tear. Instead, he viewed the place as a labor of love. He saw things that could be fixed instead of things that were broken. Boards that needed replacing he touched and marked with white chalk. Stones that required a reset, he marked, as well. Mickey spent time pulling weeds before making his way to view the field of flowers. He knew Spring would produce acres more of wildflowers. Good memories flooded back into Mickey's mind.

The men walked inside the barn.

"Mickey, there's your father-in-law's '40 Ford under a tarp if you want it," Grady told him. "It comes with the property."

***

At eighteen, Mickey saw the vehicle for the first time. One Saturday when his father brought him to see Nedra. Daniel allowed him to drive her to the end of the road and back. She'd scooted beside him, helped him drive while resting her head on his shoulder. Remembering the summery fragrance of lavender in her soft brown hair, Mickey pictured that day in his mind and smiled.

"I appreciate that, man." Mickey yanked the tarp off the truck. "Been a long time since I touched that steering wheel." He grinned, then reached for the door handle. "Think I'll climb in. With a few dollars in the motor, I know I can make it run again."

Mickey opened the truck door. Forty years of dust swarmed his face. They both laughed. His flannel shirt was covered, and face was as brown as a metal dustpan.

"I wish Nedra could see you." Grady grinned at Mickey.

"Me too." He gripped the steering wheel. "She loved this truck."

Time had faded the once comfortable and soft seat. Springs popped out of the thin and fragile cushioning. Mickey have his fiftieth vehicle, he thought. The truck needed a lot of work but held substantial sentimental value. The classic would be something to see on the streets of Savannah.

While walking the property line, Grady and Mickey heard a four-wheeler approaching on the dusty road. Mickey had a sinking feeling and slowly began to roll up his shirt sleeves. The sun beamed down harshly as a man hopped off the ATV, pistol in tow. Full of rage, the man yelled at Grady.

"Why'd you go and sell this land to Mickey Starr, Pops?" Hopping off his machine, he spat at Mickey's feet.

"Carter, this is my land, not yours!" yelled Grady. "You're not clearing this property for timber."

"The hell I ain't."

"It no longer belongs to us. Mickey can have you arrested for trespassing and should have you taken in for attempted murder. So, run along now." Grady motioned for Carter to move in the opposite direction. "Get home."

It was apparent that he had been drinking heavily with a blue ice chest strapped to the rack on his ATV. Reeking and disheveled, Carter resembled a pig rising from its wallow with sweat spots and his shirt untucked.

"Now, what are you going to do with that gun, son?"

Grady motioned for his son to hand over the gun, but Carter waved it around then pointed the gun between Mickey's eyes. The old fisherman stood solid and never flinched, which didn't go over well with Carter's bullying attempt on his uncle.

"Put... the gun... down," Mickey said calmly. "He's not going to shoot anybody, Grady. He's too scared. He'll piss on himself like when I used to watch him run from granddaddy long legs."

Carter took the butt of the rifle and struck Mickey in the face. The old man bent over in pain, grabbing his jaw and grunting.

"I have no problem shooting you in the head at close range or backing up to let the bullet zing through your heart," threatened Carter.

Stepping forward, Grady insisted, "Son, hand me the damn gun and stop screwing around!"

"No, Pops." He stepped back from Mickey. "I got something to finish with Mickey Starr."

"If he puts down the gun," said Mickey. "I can kick your son's ass for you, brother."

Grady reached out his hand.

"I'll even pay you to do it."

"Are you siding with Mickey, Pops?"

"Yeah, he's in the right, and you're a dumbass jerk!"

Mickey stepped toward Carter.

"Move another muscle, Mickey, I dare you."

Carter stared at Mickey, looking down his arm at the barrel bead pointed at his head, cocking the hammer as sweat dripped in Carter's eyes. He wiped his face and nervously took a step backward, forgetting the Heart Tree Mickey carved with his pocket knife was behind him, Carter stumbled, his trigger finger slipped.

"POW!"

"I'm hit!" shouted Mickey, grabbing his left shoulder as Grady lunged for the gun.

Carter aimed again at Mickey. Grady's feet left the ground as he turned and stretched himself across Mickey's body.

"POW! POW! POW!"

Carter climbed on his four-wheeler and took off. He knew he'd fired enough rounds to kill Mickey Starr, at least he hoped.

Mickey was hit. Just once. A flesh wound. "I'm alright," said Mickey. "You hit?"

Mickey dropped to his knees to check on his brother. Grady was on his back, hit once in the chest and once in the ribcage. One stray bullet ripped the bark on the Heart Tree.

"Mickey," said Grady, gasping for air.

"I'm right here."

Mickey knew the wound was severe. He hadn't seen blood gush like that since Korea.

"You're a good man, Mickey Starr."

"You're the better man, Grady, taking a shot like that for me."

Grady coughed.

"Two shots for your ass, and don't forget, several stab wounds, too." Grady laughed, but the pain ended the mood quickly as he gripped Mickey's hand. Blood was pouring from Grady's body.

"We need to get you to the hospital."

"You're a good brother, Mick. Glad we got to talk."

Mickey lifted his brother's head. "You're a great brother, Grady."

"Damn gunshot burns, Mick." He placed his hand on his chest. "It burns bad," Grady grunted and coughed up blood. Mickey knew it wouldn't be long as he held Grady's head.

"We're even Mick," whispered Grady, closing his eyes. "See you up there." His grip released from his brother's hand. Grady was gone.

"Stay with me, brother." He checked his eyes and pulse. Mickey screamed in anguish, "Carter, you dirty son of a bitch!"

Mickey was saddened as he realized the two only acknowledged one another as brothers, in Grady's final moments. They both knew growing up but failed to mention it. Mickey's father, Emrick, had gotten Grady's mother pregnant, but soon after, married Mickey's mother. While it was a sore spot with both families, the two never let that be a source of contention.

The neighbors heard shots, raced over to the barn and down the hill where Mickey was with Grady. Just as quickly as the altercation took place, the police search for Carter "Cigar" Johnson concluded with one count of first-degree murder, one count of attempted murder, and trespassing charges. An officer came to the hospital to deliver the good news that the suspect had been caught. Mickey thought about the handful of times he'd spent with Grady in his sixty-five years in Savannah. Sadly, the two spent most of their lives only three miles apart. Mickey wept in regret.

16

Full Moon, Full Heart

The night before Volt reported for duty, the moon was full, and the Savannah sky was clear. Shaving in the mirror, he became overwhelmed at the realization of having to say goodbye soon. One of the most memorable times of his life was now behind him. Without a doubt, no one would believe the twisted series of events that took place that month. Surely his fellow soldiers would laugh and accuse him of having an overly vivid imagination should he confide in the soldiers at the barracks.

So many lessons learned, too, Volt thought. Tipp's unwavering faith, the courage of Grady Johnson, coupled with the importance of brotherly love and living an altruistic life. And, although still painful, he learned a hard lesson about love and loss. Volt's genuine affection for Shasta plagued his mind.

Two of the bravest men he'd ever known were half-brothers. Both willing to take a bullet for the other spoke volumes to Volt due to his military affiliation. Volt decided to forgo celebrating in his honor due to the loss of Grady and with Mickey still recovering in the hospital. It just seemed untimely and inappropriate.

Mickey heard a knock at the door.

"Come in," the wounded man said, "door is open."

"Hey, Mickey, how ya feeling? I took the liberty of doing something as a thank you for all you've done for Terry and me." He looked at Mickey's shoulder but didn't say anything about his wound. "Some unfinished business I thought you might like to see."

"Can I open it? This better not be a damn prank. Some big green frog." The old man leaned his head back, grinning through the pain.

"Open it up," Volt encouraged him. "See what I brought you. I guarantee you'll like it."

Mickey needed some help releasing the ribbon, and he dropped it onto his blanket. His eyes grew large with excitement while uncapping the box.

"How did Nedra's camera survive in the weather?" he asked, with his eyes wide open. Mickey struggled to adjust his hospital bed for a better view of the box.

"Thought you might like to see these," said Volt, handing Mickey a large envelope, opening the end.

"Pictures of my tree!"

Pulling up a chair, Volt watched his friend wipe his eyes. Mickey pressed his lips together, refraining from crying as his eyes flooded with tears. He sat quietly for a moment, staring at the top picture, unable to move.

"The film survived," said Mickey. "All thirty-six pictures printed."

Wildflower fields and horses were nibbling grass in the shadows of the oaks. Each photo revealed such beautiful scenery. Mickey continued flipping through the stack of photographs, pausing at a picture of the initial laden tree, clutching it to his chest.

"Keep going, Mickey," encouraged Volt.

"I'm taking my time. Don't rush me."

Mickey shuffled carefully through the pictures when suddenly, he froze and gasped.

"I bet you didn't know that one was on the role of film, did ya?"

"That's Nedra and me. Look at her long hair. She's beautiful." He lifted the hospital bed higher. "Oh, what a beautiful, beautiful soul."

Tears slowly streamed down Mickey's cheeks as the old man sniffed and wiped the wetness away with his gown sleeve.

"She was radiant, Mick," Volt noted. "How old was that roll of film?"

"Must have been just before she got sick, I guess." His hands were shaking as he separated the photographs his way. "Look at her. There we are having breakfast together in Hilton Head. She loved a morning cup of brew."

Mickey stared at the pictures and smiled. His lips moved, but no words came, thumbing back through them again and again. His eyes had a unique glow. His face curled a smile in relief, and he was content, it appeared.

"Thanks, Volt," replied Mickey, tapping on the top of the box. "This means the world to me. You will be on my mind when you are overseas. I'll be praying for you when you get deployed. You can bet on it." Mickey shook his hand in appreciation of the gift.

Volt stood and walked to the door. Mickey saluted his friend and glanced back at a picture of Nedra before closing his eyes to nap.

***

Volt examined the Savannah sky as he trekked back to Mickey's to gather his things and head out. Making a quick stop at the neighbors, Volt knocked on the door.

"Hi, Mr. McGregor. Is Shasta home?"

With a stern look, he examined the soldier. "She's home," lifting his chin, crossed his arms. "But I think she made it clear that she doesn't want to see you."

"Just five minutes, sir?" pleading his case. "Mr. McGregor, please. I'm being deployed."

"Not tonight. I'll let Shasta know you stopped by, though. Be safe on the frontlines."

Mr. McGregor shut the door and walked away.

The soldier wasn't the type of man to just give up. Volt struggled to stay positive. He grabbed his guitar and headed to the back patio, hoping she would hear him playing and walk out to the Wilmington River beside him. Music was Volt's weapon of choice. As predicted, he played, and the door opened. Volt turned and stood up, hoping she would give him a few minutes.

"One question," she shouted, "did you kiss Brandi at the bar?"

"I did, I admit it, I kissed Brandi."

He dropped his head and pretended to tinker with his guitar, attempting to avoid her laser beam eyes.

"Well, Volt, that's unfortunate," she snapped her head away and pretended he wasn't there.

"I'm sorry. I'm not even going to give you a list of reasons that will take the heat off of me." He sat his guitar by his side. "I just need to know what we do now? I can't leave with us on bad terms." Volt cocked his head sideways and awkwardly glanced at Shasta. "I'm sorry and sickened that it hurt your feelings."

The soldier eased closer to her side, taking a few steps away from the riverbank.

"Don't come over here and try to sweet talk me," she demanded while fighting back the tears. Shasta wiped her eyes, and Volt walked up close enough to put his arms around her.

"I hurt you. I was wrong and stupid. You may not believe this about me, but that's not my typical behavior. I just don't make it a habit of..."

"Moving on so quickly!"

Shasta was torn between anger and sadness.

A lump of regret started to form in Volt's throat, "I don't want her. I want you. Can we start over?" he pleaded.

"I'm not sure I can ever trust you." She looked up at Volt. Broken-hearted, her mascara ran a trail down her face. Volt took the tail of his shirt and patted her cheeks.

"I bought you something." He unfolded his hand. "Open it."

She gently flipped up the small box lid. "This is beautiful, but I can't accept this. I'm not there yet. I am angry about the kiss and embarrassed too."

"I know you're hurting. And I couldn't be more regretful and sorry. I promise I'll make it up to you. Please? Please? Shasta, please?" Volt reached for her hand. "Shasta, I give you my word and my life."

He slowly took the ring box from her and removed the single diamond ring. Dropping the empty box onto the rock patio, Volt bent down on one knee. Gazing into her tear-filled eyes, he asked, "Shasta, you're the only girl I want. I only want you for the rest of my life." He began to place the ring on her finger. "This is yours to keep. I hope you will wear it and not chuck it into the bottom of the river or your jewelry box. Say yes, Shasta and I'll be the luckiest man alive. Say you'll wear it?"

"Are you asking me to marry you?"

"Yes ma'am, I'm sure I did," curling his famous smile. "But you haven't answered." Volt fidgeted on the hard-stone surface of the patio. "Shasta, I'm sorry, and I've apologized. Not proud of how I've made you feel. But I'm genuine with my request and sincere with how I feel for you." He held her hands. "Shasta McGregor, I am asking you to spend the rest of your life with me despite what has happened and what others might say. I want you to give me your heart because I've already given you mine."

"Volt, I, I, I, I just can't." Shasta's words pierced his heart. She shook her head. "I'm not going to be your back up plan or one of your means of entertainment while you're deployed. That's not me. I'm tender and warm, and loyal. I deserve to feel special and to be made a priority." She dropped her head. "I don't want to be with someone whose actions make me second guess myself or make me feel second class in my heart. I don't want to marry someone who makes my mascara smear and my heartbreak when another lady walks up for a dance or a kiss from a star singer."

"I deserve that. I'm heartbroken, but I've got no one to blame but myself. The offer still stands. Maybe you'll find it in you to forgive me, or find it in you to love me."

"I do love you, Volt," moving her hand. "It's a beautiful ring, but I cannot accept it." Shasta pulled the ring from her finger and placed it in Volt's shirt pocket.

"Can I at least write to you and call when I can?"

"Of course, I'd love to hear from you. I still care about you and your safety. Let's keep in touch. I'll always love you."

"So, there's a chance?"

"Don't press your luck, Mr. Hendricks."

"Yes, Mrs. Hendricks," Volt kidded and smiled.

Shasta rolled her eyes with a sly smile, waving as she walked to her backdoor. Volt stood still and watched her walk away, picking up his guitar.

***

KNOCK, KNOCK, KNOCK. Volt wildly clanged the door knocker. "Hello, Mrs. McGregor, could I see Shasta?" Volt spoke with confidence when she answered the door.

"Again?"

"Please ma'am, I'm sorry to bother you, but could you please ask Shasta to come see me?"

"Shasta!" turning and looking upstairs, "You have a visitor," she shouted. "It's the singer again!"

Shasta appeared at the top of the stairs and rolled her eyes. "What? Not you again. We'll step outside to talk?"

She descended the stairs, and the lovers moved toward the back patio for privacy. She assumed it was time for his final goodbye before leaving town.

When the couple came to a nice spot, Volt nervously spoke. "I'm being sincere. Hear me out, please."

"Okay, then, talk. Have you given Brandi her goodbye kiss yet?"

"Nope. That's not going to happen."

Volt touched her hand. She responded with a squeeze from both of her hands as they faced each other.

"I'm in love with you," he said with a low tone. "You're hurt and mad. And understandably so."

"Yeah, Volt, I get it. We've gone over this, I forgive you. I just need time to think about the ring and you. And whether this is something I want in my life or not?"

"I'm asking for one more chance to make this work. Can we do that?" Volt leaned in to caress her. Shasta pushed him away. He pulled the ring from his pocket. "I love you. I want to spend the rest of my life with you. Shasta Kaye McGregor, will you marry me?"

"You're so persistent."

"Well, I'm gonna keep asking until I get the answer I want from you." His face turned a happy grin.

Placing one hand on her waist and cocking out her hip, Shasta extended her left hand. "Fine, then. Yes, I'll marry you. But Volt Hendricks, if you ever make me cry again, I'll tell my daddy on you. He and Mickey Starr will drop you out in the middle of the Atlantic Ocean."

"I'd just swim back to you. You'll only cry happy tears from here on out."

Slipping the ring back onto her finger, Volt whispered, "I love you. I promise you'll never regret saying yes. How about you and I drive to town and celebrate our engagement?"

Tipp started backing out of Mickey's driveway when he spotted the two next door. He stopped and threw a hand out of the window to wave, then continued down the long driveway.

Shasta's face lit up at the sudden realization, "We're getting married!"

"Congratulations!" shouted Tipp.

They kissed, and neither one of them wanted to let go.

"Volt, let's borrow a bottle from Mickey's cellar to celebrate. George will let us in."

Walking down to Mickey's wine cellar, Shasta noticed that her ring was heavy and bounced with each step. Volt opened the door to the cool room.

"Wow." He examined a large array of wines from across the world. "I have never seen anything like this before." Volt raked his finger along some of the titles. "You'll have to pick one because I'm lost. My mind is only familiar with breweries."

"Okay, this one," Shasta said, pulling a bottle from the wall.

The lovers asked George for glasses and proceeded to walk up the stairs to Volt's room.

"I'll freshen up in the lady's room." Shasta excused herself as Volt uncorked the bottle and poured the wine. When she returned from behind the door, she was wearing a guest robe.

"I love the white robe, but it's a little big on you."

"I'm trying to be romantic here, could you just play along? You are blowing my introduction. Keep quiet." Peeling the robe off her shoulders, she let it drop to the floor.

"You are stunning."

Volt pulled the blankets from the top corner of the bed and motioned for her to get comfortable. As Shasta climbed into bed, Volt undressed then joined her. He massaged her shoulders then slid her long brown hair to one side, exposing her neckline. Volt touched her skin softly and eased his way down the front of her body.

Grabbing his hand, Shasta called his name, "Volt. Wait. Please don't be mad." Volt returned to kissing her neckline. "Volt, I can't. It's too soon."

"Are you alright?"

Volt asked with concern.

"You drive me crazy; you know that?" She pulled his face toward hers. "But I can't do this, at least not right now. Just hold me."

Volt lost his smile. Disappointed, he obliged his bride to be.

"I'm going to miss you," she confessed, kissing and pulling him tighter.

"I don't want to ever let you go," he said, kissing her shoulder. "I love you."

"I love you too. The ring is beautiful."

Shasta spun the gold around her finger and admired the size of the diamond, bending her hand with pride. The couple spent the rest of the day together, laughing and cuddling. Talking about the future. Walking about the property, they examined Mickey's car collection. As they toured the cars, Shasta felt enveloped with emotion and succumbed to Volt's affection as the two made love in the backseat in one of the old man's cars. Shasta found herself feeling uninhibited with Volt as she smiled and breathed a sigh of relief.

"I gotta go," he nodded. "Shasta, babe, it's time for me to report for duty."

Resting her head on Volt's shoulder, the two gathered his things and packed up his truck. They kissed and cried and embraced until the tangerine sun set over Whitemarsh Island. She held her hands over her mouth as he slowly backed out of the driveway. Suddenly, the vehicle's brakes squealed as the truck came to a halt. The soldier jumped from the truck and began to run back towards her. Scooping her up into his arms, Volt professed, "I love you with all my heart and soul."

"I believe you."

After one last passionate kiss, Volt returned to the truck and drove to Fort Stewart, Georgia, where he deployed.

17

The Most Beautiful Place

Six months have passed since Mickey purchased Nedra's property from Grady. Mickey spent every waking moment working to restore the house to its former beauty. The transition from fisherman to carpenter caused Mickey to fall out of love with fishing just long enough to pass the business on to Tipp and officially retire. His joints and bones hurt at bedtime, but he was proud of the progress in restoring the property, which became a labor of love. The owner of the Tobacco Barn soon found contentment in a job that would prove no financial gain. He enjoyed the peaceful satisfaction that it brought him, a new life, and one he'd forgotten existed. A gentle breeze off the coast kept the fields in motion. Viewed from the soft clouds above, he predicted Nedra could see the wide-open fields and work he'd done to make the home as close to what he'd known when he first met her.

The better part of the cold winter, Mickey parted with the superfluous things in his life. He sold his house in Whitemarsh Island and took only essentials and memories with him to the house on Tobacco Road. Tipp couldn't understand his sudden urge to downsize and liquidate now that finances were no longer an issue. The old man discovered solace in passing along assets that would bring joy to others. From a fine bottle of wine to an automobile, Mickey sold and gifted most of what he'd spent his whole life collecting.

While his drinking had slowed substantially, his pipe was working overtime. Terry stayed behind and made a decent living between helping Mickey at the barn and assisting Tipp with the boat repairs. The old farm was breathing new life again, and Mickey sat on the porch, enjoying a glass of sweet tea. A car he didn't recognize pulled into the driveway. He stood from the rocking chair when a gorgeous young lady stepped from the car and approached him.

"Hey, Mickey!"

"Shasta McGregor! Get up here and give me a hug. Where have you been keeping yourself?"

"It's good to see you," she said, kissing his cheek and hugging the old man.

"Great to see you. What are you doing out this way, doll?" Mickey moved his rocking chair closer to hear her speak.

"Well, I have a big favor to ask of you."

"What's that?"

"Mom thought it would be nice if we had the wedding here at the Tobacco Barn, and I agreed. It's beautiful out here. I just love it."

"Shasta, I'd be offended if you didn't have it here," he grinned.

"You are the best, Mickey Starr. More generous than any man I've ever known."

"Well, thank you for your kind words. How's Volt doing, by the way?"

"He calls when he can, but he can't share too much."

"Is he going to re-enlist?"

"I don't think so," she shook her head. "He's wanting to come home and focus on his music a little more and write a few songs. But who knows?"

Mickey held her hand, comforting the bride-to-be.

"I know it's hard, seeing all that stuff about war on television and in the newspapers."

"Yeah, makes it difficult to sleep most nights, but I just try to stay busy during the days and wear myself out," she explained.

"I hope he gets home soon. When do you expect him back in Savannah?"

She stared across the yard to a nearby field and watched the horses pace.

"Well, if all goes as planned, he'll take leave for the wedding during the first week in June. But with a war going on..."

"A June wedding? Good, gives me a little more time to get the place ready."

"Oh no, please don't go to any trouble. It's perfect right now!"

"The pictures will be beautiful. You know, pictures help keep the good memories alive," he added, reflecting on Nedra.

"Well, I hate to 'beg and bolt' as my daddy calls it when I come into town." The two shared a laugh. "But I have a meeting I need to get to in Savannah. What you are doing is wonderful, and we are gracious. You are like a grandfather to me. It was so good to see you." Shasta waved as she stepped from the front steps and made her way back to the car.

"Just tell me what color horse and carriage you want," Mickey called out.

"Will do," Shasta replied from the car window.

Mickey stood up and yelled, "Hey, Shasta. Can you wait a minute? I've got something I need to give you." Shasta shifted her car back into park and released her seatbelt to get out. Making her way toward the house, Mickey came out with a manilla envelope and handed it to her. "It's an early wedding gift, but promise me that you won't open it until you get back to your parents' house," Mickey pleaded as he handed her the large envelope.

"Sure, no problem, and thank you in advance for the wonderful surprise."

The bride-to-be took the envelope from his grasp, once again climbed into the vehicle, and drove off. Arriving at her parents' home, Shasta eagerly peeked into the envelope, finding a large stack of cash and a note:

For making memories.

Love,

Mickey

"I'm speechless." Shasta sat in her car, thumbing through the dollar bills as tears streamed down her face. Leaning her head against the headrest of the vehicle, Shasta lowered the visor mirror to wipe away the tears and fix her face. Her tears turned to joy, shrieking in delight. Clambering to get out of the car to tell her parents about Mickey's wedding fund, Shasta neglected to unhook her seatbelt. Swinging her arms wildly and looking as if she was caught in a spider's web, Shasta howled at how silly she must appear.

***

Mickey once thought he was a generous man because he would share his allusive lifestyle with his friends and family. Now, Mickey realized that a truly generous man doesn't share; a generous man gives things of importance away.

Terry and Mickey spent the remainder of the weeks preparing the Tobacco Barn for a wedding complete with arches and gazebos for a picturesque view. They even added a shelter should the rain decide to roll in from the coast.

All of a sudden, Terry plowed across the porch nearing Mickey.

"Mickey, did you see the bullet holes in the front door of the Tobacco Barn?" The two men sprinted to the barn to investigate. Terry ran his fingers across the damage.

"Who the hell did this?" Mickey touched the wooden barn doors.

Fire raced through his blood as he opened the swinging doors to the barn. Terry and Mickey scampered out to the truck to drive around the property and scope it out.

"The wedding is in three days," said Mickey. "Some jackass is running around being destructive, trying to mess with us."

"My first guess would be Carter "Cigar" Johnson," said Terry, "but he's still in jail. Who else would seek retaliation?"

Mickey thought and answered, "I don't know, but maybe Magnum Frisco. He was in on trying to jump Tipp and Volt in Hilton Head not too long ago.

"Volt flies in tomorrow morning. I don't want him settling any business on his wedding weekend. He's seen enough turmoil, at war. The soldier doesn't need any more added drama right now."

Terry was serious about trying to keep the dust settled for his brother and let him enjoy the wedding.

"This is a dead-end road, so if they come back," said Mickey, pointing at the driveway. "We will have them trapped. Just need to keep our eyes peeled."

Mickey and Terry finished scouting as far as the truck would allow them to travel before heading back to the house.

"If they come back to the Tobacco Barn," Terry pounded on the barn, "we'll be ready for them."

***

Terry picked Volt up from the airport. Despite risking Volt's wedding weekend, he spilled the beans about the bullet holes and the possibility of Magnum Frisco making an uninvited appearance to the Tobacco Barn again. Terry was worried about friends and family from North Carolina driving down for the wedding and finding themselves amidst a hornet's nest.

Mickey was worried about Volt, he seemed uneasy about something, and rightly so, he was still concerned for the boy.

"Volt, you okay?" asked Mickey. "What's going on, man? Second thoughts? Nerves?"

Volt straddled the cedar and spoke softly.

"Nervous, yeah, maybe."

Mickey confided in him, grinning, and laughing, "It's not unusual for a man to have jitters before his big day. Are you gonna be alright?"

"Yeah. Between the war, the wedding details, my label, and Shasta," said Volt, sweating. "Now this joker, Magnum, who shot up the barn, it's just a lot to take in. My job is uncertain, I can't make plans that I can promise to fulfill, and Shasta, who is planning every facet of my life from exiting the Army to baby names. It's, uh, well, I'm overloaded."

"Listen, most of that stuff is just girls dreaming out loud mixed with a little wishful thinking," Mickey explained, trying to console him. "Do you love her?"

"I do," Volt said with assurance.

"Then get ready for your bachelor's party tonight," Mickey ordered. "Ease this silliness from your mind."

"You're going with us, aren't you?"

"Heck no!" He retorted, "Not me. I am staying right here. And I hope it's not in the Savannah Morning News, either," laughing.

***

Now that Mickey was home alone, he began executing a plan. The old man jumped in his truck and drove to the far end of a long straight stretch. Backing the truck into a narrow hiding spot, Mickey settled in out of view from other vehicles.

Mosquitoes buzzed as he waited with the window down, enjoying the gentle evening breeze on Tobacco Road. An owl hooted in a nearby tree and crickets chirped as he checked his wristwatch, leaning forward, Mickey could see headlights headed in his direction.

Once the driver parked, there was more than one person nosing around. Struggling to focus with his aging sight, Mickey noticed one of the men appeared to be struggling to carry something. He waited to see what the men were going to do.

"That's a gas drum!"

Realizing what was about to unfold, Mickey punched the accelerator on his truck and headed for the barn. POOF! Flames and smoke shot through the air as the front of the barn was ablaze, out of control. Struggling to think about how to fight the fire, Mickey anticipated a different type of battle. Three cop cars slung gravel in all directions, beating him to the barn, before surrounding the property and the trespassers. He parked and scrambled to find a water hose as his faithful neighbors called the fire department. The old man sauntered over to identify the arsonists as a fire truck unloaded and began pumping water on the front doors of the blazing barn.

"Thank you for the favor," added Mickey. "Now, I can get some sleep tonight."

Officer Jay Herndon returned, "I'll keep you posted, but I don't think you're gonna have anything further to worry about from here on out. Well, except for building a new set of barn doors next week. Sorry, buddy."

The policeman shook Mickey's hand and followed another car to the station to book the suspects of the Tobacco Barn fire.

***

Tipp was the designated driver for the night, and just before sun up, they all crashed at Mickey's farmhouse. Tired and nauseous, the group headed straight to bed. Hearing the boys come in, Mickey waited until mid-morning to wake the crew.

"Hey, boys?" shouted Mickey. "I need y'all to get up. It's important. I'll meet you in the kitchen with coffee and a truckload of aspirin."

"Good morning, Mickey," said Volt. "This is my Army buddy, Tyler Goodwater." The two shook hands. "What's going on?"

"Good to meet you, Mr. Starr," said Tyler, who washed his hands. "Breakfast smells good."

Mickey poured Tyler and Volt coffee, stacking ham biscuits and bacon on the table for the soldiers.

Tipp and Terry sleepily staggered down the stairs.

"Guys, I'm gonna need you to get some coffee," said Mickey. "Get your shoes on and meet me at the barn in five minutes." Mickey solicited them with a serious face.

"Yes, sir," the men replied.

"What in the hell happened here?" demanded the groom.

"Was this an accident?" asked Terry.

"Who did this?" asked Tipp. "Was it Magnum?"

"Nope." Mickey returned, examining the doors in the daylight.

"The Bull River Boys?" asked Volt.

"Nope," Mickey continued to answer.

"Did Carter send someone from jail?" asked Terry.

"It was Brandi and a friend of hers seeking revenge on Shasta for marrying Volt." Mickey walked in front of the men to elaborate on the story. "They gassed the place, struck a match, and watched it burn, in a devil's blaze."

"Mickey!" yelled Volt. "Damn it, I'm frickin' sick to my stomach over this. I'll pay for it and build it back myself." He punched the doors and cussed to himself.

"Listen, that's what insurance is for," said Mickey. "I'm not worried about the cost, I'm worried about the bride, raising hell," he said without hesitation.

Turning to Mickey, Volt panicked, "Does Shasta know?"

"Heck no, Shasta doesn't know anything about the barn yet," Mickey assured him.

"But you better believe she'll be here in a few hours," warned the groom. "She's gonna flip out and cry if we don't get to work. I can't believe her cousin tried to burn the barn down," said Volt, slamming the doors. This can't be happening on the day of our wedding. Shasta is going to kill me!"

"Well men, let's fix this before the boss comes," Mickey teased, handing out tools to each man.

Together, they scrubbed, sawed, and nailed for hours. Mickey took several bales of hay and spread it over the ground to keep Shasta's dress from the mud and charred ground from the firetruck. Exhausted and filthy, the men went inside to eat and shower.

"You think Raquel will make us some crepes while she's here?" asked Tipp, missing her cooking, especially now that she'd relocated to Orlando.

"Boy, Raquel doesn't have time to make you something to eat; she's busy catering the wedding," said Mickey. "Make yourself a peanut butter sandwich and don't bother her," ordered the old man.

***

Volt sent word to Shasta about what had happened, but made her promise that she wouldn't come out to see the damage until they had a chance to repair the doors. Shasta was beside herself with anger toward Brandi.

Mickey had the neighbor's horses staged at the fence, like a Kentucky horse race or something out of a Southern equestrian magazine. A line of chestnut and light bay thoroughbreds hung their heads over the fence adjacent to Mickey's property as if they were asked to do so, and yet it was a rare coincidence. The long, white wedding carriage was rolled off a flatbed trailer where the handler bridled the horse for the bride and groom. Guests were beginning to arrive, so Mickey went to check on Volt.

"How's it going, lover boy?" Mickey teased Volt, offering his hand in honor of his big day. "Are you ready for your vows?"

Volt chuckled. "Not so bad, I guess."

"How are you, buddy?" asked Mark, standing tall and straight as a Georgia pine.

Mickey caught Volt with his back turned, talking with his groomsmen, so he tucked a thick envelope into his tuxedo jacket pocket, hanging on a chair in the rear of the barn.

"Enjoy this, Volt," said Mickey. "If you are a blessed man, you'll never have to do it again," he stated, "'til death do you part."

"That's what I'm banking on."

"A man should marry his best friend." Mickey stuffed his hands in his pockets, excusing himself from the room. "The minister would like to see you."

"Send him in," waved Volt.

The wedding planner knocked on the door notifying the men that it was time. The groom grabbed his tuxedo jacket, and the heaviness of the coat alerted him to check his pockets. A white business envelope with the Starr Fishing Company logo held a hefty stack of cash, two airline tickets, bound by a note:

Volt,

Make some memories.

Love,

Mickey

***

Volt ran after Mickey to thank him for the honeymoon fund and the tickets.

"Oh yeah, I almost forgot." Mickey held out his hand. "Here, I found this in the backseat of my black Ford Model-A Tudor." Mickey opened his hand, returning Volt's gold watch.

The young man smiled, remembering that special day with Shasta as if it just happened.

"Oh, I wondered where I left it," grinning and laughing as he remembered the day. "Please don't ask me how it got there." Volt snapped the watch on his wrist. "This watch was given to me by my grandfather."

Volt was thrilled to have it back in his possession and was just as happy to see that Mickey didn't make a big deal about where he'd found it.

The men made their way to the barn. Soon after, the music started.

"Please rise," requested the pastor. The crowd turned as rays of sunlight beamed through the bullet holes in the barn doors.

"Like a ray of hope," whispered Mickey.

Tipp winked at his grandfather. "Look," pointing at the rays of bright sunlight beaming through the holes in the barn. The doors slowly swung open wide, building the anticipation of Volt witnessing his beautiful bride.

A collective swoon swept over the audience as Mr. McGregor escorted Shasta into the barn. Volt stood staring at her beauty and was overcome with emotion. Perhaps a result of exhaustion, being a little hungover, or typical wedding jitters. Volt was entranced by her, elated and smiling as stunning Shasta made her way down the aisle. In that moment, rare as the sunlight through the door earlier, he was confident in his decision to marry her. The sun-kissed face of the bride was glowing pure radiance as she pulled her ivory dress and took her place beside him. Her brown wavy hair was loosely pinned up, exposing a single strand of her mother's pearls, draped across her neck, and her matching earrings were like stars plucked from the sky.

Volt whispered in her ear, "You look beautiful, babe."

Shasta smiled and winked at him. "I was hoping you'd be pleased."

With his arms crossed, Mickey stood to the side, quietly overcome with the love and loss of his bride, hoping that Volt would share the same passion for Shasta as he did for Nedra. Here, he was flooded by an overwhelming sense of peace and calmness that made him feel closer to God than he'd ever felt. Mickey closed his eyes and whispered a quiet prayer.

After the ceremony, Volt and Shasta were instructed to climb aboard the custom-made long, white princess wedding carriage that would bring them to their final wedding surprise. After a quick trip, the carriage stopped where Mickey had a car waiting for his favorite newlyweds. Volt laughed out loud when he realized that Mickey was gifting them with his black Ford Model-A Tudor. The car where they had first surrendered their love to one another. The car where Volt removed his watch in the back seat, and where Mickey saw the groom's name engraved on the back of the case.

Volt hoisted his happy bride from the princess carriage with the utmost gentleness, leading her to settle into the front seat of the newly restored Ford Model-A Tudor. Taking a seat on the driver's side, Volt grabbed the wheel, honked the horn, and started the car. Shasta slid across the seat next to him, resting her head on his shoulder as the two drove down Tobacco Road, in love.

Mickey bade goodnight to the final guests. Turning off the last light with the string from the center of the barn where he married Nedra decades earlier, he skipped across the hay strewn path to the farmhouse. Mickey showered and dressed for bed. Shortly after lying down, he drifted off into a sound and peaceful sleep, dreaming of his life with Nedra. She gave him a big bear hug and kissed his lips. Together they walked and held hands before resting on a blanket in an endless field of wildflowers. Mickey brewed her favorite coffee with a pitcher of water from her daddy's spring. A knock on the front door took Mickey away from making coffee.

"Come on in, Grady," waved Mickey. "Nedra's making breakfast."

Mickey closed the door and followed Grady to the kitchen.

"Good morning, Grady," said Nedra. "Care for some coffee?"

Grabbing an extra mug from the hutch, Mickey asked, "Grady, what do you take in your coffee?"

Grady grinned slyly, "Cream and sugar, Sugar."

The brothers laughed as Nedra wrapped her arms around Mickey, placing her head against his chest. "I love you, Mickey. I knew I'd see you again, someday."

***

"Hello? Hello?" called Tipp. "Anyone home?"

Tipp continued calling out as he scoured the house looking for his Grandpa. Surprised by Tipp's voice, Mickey lept from the bed and made his way to the top of the stairs.

"I'm here, Tipp," Mickey yelled down to him. "Be down in a bit."

Mickey dressed and met Tipp in the kitchen, and his first thought as he rushed downstairs, was Nedra saying, "Cream and sugar, Sugar." What he wouldn't give to hear her say that one more time?

"Must have been some dance party after I left last night, you're still in bed." Tipp sat at the kitchen table. "I knocked on the door for five minutes."

Mickey stood confused, hoping Nedra would walk through the house with her daddy's coffee-water and fresh-cut flowers in her hand. No coffee was brewing, and sadly, no Nedra either. Tipp scampered around the kitchen for a quick bite to eat.

"Would you like me to get you a sandwich, Mr. Tipp?" offered George. "I'm not as good as Raquel, but I can make a mean BLT."

"Oh, yes sir, George," Tipp answered, pouring his orange juice. "Can you make it two sandwiches?" said Tipp. "I'll take them to go, please."

Mickey placed his hand on the wall to steady himself as Tipp and George buzzed about the kitchen. Taking in a long deep breath, Mickey smiled with contentment as he recalled last night's vivid imagery. So real as if he lived it. Closing his eyes, he thanked God for the reunion with his wife, even if for a short moment, made him miss her that much more. The sound of a car pulling into the driveway stirred Mickey back into reality as he looked out the kitchen window. The men made their way to the front porch to greet the lady.

"Come on in, Hadley," invited Mickey.

"Wow!" This place is incredible," said Hadley, as she examined the beautiful view from the swing. "I'm sorry I didn't make it to the wedding last night. I just flew in this morning from Charlotte," she explained.

Tipp grabbed the lunches from George and snatched his grandmother's throw from the back of the sofa.

"Hadley came over to walk the trails and ride the Friesian horses," said Tipp.

"And have a picnic lunch under the Heart Tree," said the radiant lady with emerald eyes and an unforgettable smile.

Reaching into his pants pocket, Mickey pulled out his father's pocket knife and tucked it into Tipp's hand, and said, "Looks like you're gonna need this."

Hadley saw what Mickey had done.

"No one can carve out a love story better than you, Mickey Starr," said Hadley.

"She's a rare jewel," replied Mickey. "Go carve your own love story."

Later, the glowing light of of the Savannah sky dimmed, fading from orange and blue and purple into a starry night, stretched across the coastal horizon, like the paint whisk across a pearl white canvas as the velvet night fell over the silhouette of the Tobacco Barn, Mickey was without regret.

After a delightful evening of laughing at Mickey's stories, Hadley sang like an angel in a gospel choir, song after song in perfection until she could sing no more. Handling the harmonica like a professional Mickey played while Tipp and Hadley danced on the front lawn in the light of a silver moon until her sandals were dusty and worn and then Tipp drove her home. George and Mickey sang one together, echoing with vibrant voices, and George called it a night.

Around midnight, sitting alone on the front porch, Mickey reminisced about his love for Nedra; the fire still burning inside from their memories. He knew what it meant to be relentless; to win, lose and love. Tipp had shared his faith with him in his darkest moments. Finally understanding his newly discovered faith, made Mickey hopeful, with less presentiment, for himself as well as others.

About the Author

In 2017, after a professor at Liberty University suggested one of Pete's stories be made into a film. Inspired by what she said, Pete traveled to Savannah, Georgia, where he outlined the idea to write his first novel, *The Tobacco Barn*. Pete is an avid painter and traveler who enjoys southern fiction. In 2018, Pete's manuscript of *The Tobacco Barn* was accepted by the Romance Writers of America. He is a member of The Hemingway Society. Pete lives in North Carolina with his wife and his two sons, both with autism. This story was written to honor the spiritual journey of his grandfather, Clifford "Tippie" Lester.

The Tobacco Barn is the first of **The Hearts & Heroes Series.** Pete's next novel, *Saddles of Barringer* will be published in the latter part of 2020, and his third book, *Andy Oliver* will be in 2021. Follow him on social media for updates.

Pete Lester uses the pen name Tennessee Gunns.

Follow new titles by Pete Lester on social media:

Website - tennesseegunnsnovel.com

Facebook - Tennessee Gunns Novel

Twitter - https://twitter.com/pete_media

Pinterest - https://www.pinterest.com/TennesseeGunns123/

Instagram -
https://www.instagram.com/tennesseegunnsnovel/

LinkedIn - https://www.linkedin.com/in/pete-lester-phd-709bb7124

Graciously Sponsored by:

Tasty Pickles by Carson

Carson's Story

Carson has a passion for PICKLES! He also has autism and is learning disabled. When thinking about his future, Carson feared that he would never be able to get a job. His crippling anxiety about the future and dread of limited workforce abilities encouraged him to begin thinking about being his own boss. Inspired by a school project, Carson started his own pickle business. Carson's pickle adventure has given him an incredible sense of pride and has helped him to not only grow in confidence but to also improve both academically and socially. We are thrilled for Carson and his success! Our hope is that Carson's story will help others find their niche in life and hearten others to believe in and support DIFFERENT-ABLED individuals.

www.tastypicklesbycarson.com

tastypicklesbycarson@gmail.com

www.ingramcontent.com/pod-product-compliance
Lightning Source LLC
Chambersburg PA
CBHW070005120726
47909CB00003B/810